PUCK OF POOK'S HILL

CHILDREN'S
CLASSICS

PUCK OF POOK'S HILL

Rudyard Kipling

Bloomsbury Books
London

This edition published 1994 by Bloomsbury Books, an
imprint of The Godfrey Cave Group, 42 Bloomsbury Street,
London, WC1B 3QJ.

ISBN 1 85471 203 9

Printed and bound by Firmin-Didot (France),
Group Herissey. No d'impression : 27841.

Contents

Weland's Sword

See you the dimpled track that runs,
  All hollow through the wheat?
O that was where they hauled the guns
  That smote King Philip's fleet!

See you our little mill that clacks,
  So busy by the brook?
She has ground her corn and paid her tax
  Ever since Domesday Book.

See you our stilly woods of oak,
  And the dread ditch beside?
O that was where the Saxons broke,
  On the day that Harold died!

See you the windy levels spread
  About the gates of Rye?
O that was where the Northmen fled,
  When Alfred's ships came by!

See you our pastures wide and lone,
  Where the red oxen browse?
O there was a City thronged and known,
  Ere London boasted a house!

And see you, after rain, the trace
  Of mound and ditch and wall?

O that was a Legion's camping place,
  When Caesar sailed from Gaul!

And see you marks that show and fade,
  Like shadows on the Downs?
O they are the lines the Flint Men made,
  To guard their wondrous towns!

Trackway and Camp and City lost,
  Salt Marsh where now is corn;
Old Wars, old Peace, old Arts that cease,
  And so was England born!

She is not any common Earth,
  Water or Wood or Air,
But Merlin's Isle of Gramarye,
  Where you and I will fare.

The children were at the Theatre, acting to Three Cows as much as they could remember of *Midsummer Night's Dream.* Their father had made them a small play out of the big Shakespeare one, and they had rehearsed it with him and with their mother till they could say it by heart. They began when Nick Bottom the weaver comes out of the bushes with a donkey's head on his shoulders, and finds Titania, Queen of the Fairies, asleep. Then they skipped to the part where Bottom asks three little fairies to scratch his head and bring him honey, and they ended where he falls asleep in Titania's arms. Dan was Puck and Nick Bottom, as well as all three Fairies. He wore a pointy-eared cloth cap for Puck, and a paper donkey's head out of a Christmas cracker – but it tore if you were not careful – for Bottom. Una was Titania, with a wreath of columbines and a foxglove wand.

The Theatre lay in a meadow called the Long Slip. A little mill-stream, carrying water to a mill two or three fields away, bent round one corner of it, and in the middle of the bend lay a large old Fairy Ring of darkened grass, which was the stage. The mill-stream banks, overgrown with willow, hazel, and guelder-rose, made convenient places to wait in till your turn came; and a grown-up who had seen it said that Shakespeare himself could not have imagined a more suitable setting for his play. They were not, of course, allowed to act on Midsummer Night itself, but they went down after tea on Midsummer Eve, when the shadows were growing, and they took their supper – hard-boiled eggs, Bath Oliver biscuits, and salt in an envelope – with them. Three Cows had been milked and were grazing steadily with a tearing noise that one could hear all down the meadow; and the noise of the Mill at work sounded like bare feet running on hard ground. A cuckoo sat on a gate-post singing his broken June tune, "cuckoo-cuck", while a busy kingfisher crossed from the millstream, to the brook which ran on the other side of the meadow. Everything else was a sort of thick, sleepy stillness smelling of meadow-sweet and dry grass.

Their play went beautifully. Dan remembered all his parts – Puck, Bottom, and the three Fairies – and Una never forgot a word of Titania – not even the difficult piece where she tells the Fairies how to feed Bottom with "apricocks, green figs, and dewberries", and all the lines end in "ies". They were both so pleased that they acted it three times over from beginning to end before they sat down in the unthistly centre of the Ring to eat eggs and Bath Olivers. This was when they heard a whistle among the alders on the bank, and they jumped.

The bushes parted. In the very spot where Dan had stood as Puck they saw a small, brown, broad-shouldered, pointy-eared person with a snub nose, slanting blue eyes, and a grin that ran right across his freckled face. He shaded his forehead as though he were watching Quince, Snout, Bottom, and the others rehearsing *Pyramus and Thisbe,* and, in a voice as deep as Three Cows asking to be milked, he began:

> "What hempen homespuns have we swaggering here,
> So near the cradle of the fairy Queen?"

He stopped, hollowed one hand round his ear, and, with a wicked twinkle in his eye, went on:

> "What, a play toward? I'll be an auditor;
> An actor, too, perhaps, if I see cause."

The children looked and gasped. The small thing – he was no taller than Dan's shoulder – stepped quietly into the Ring.

"I'm rather out of practice," said he; "but that's the way my part ought to be played."

Still the children stared at him – from his dark-blue cap, like a big columbine flower, to his bare, hairy feet. At last he laughed.

"Please don't look like that. It isn't *my* fault. What else could you expect?" he said.

"We didn't expect any one," Dan answered slowly. "This is our field."

"Is it?" said their visitor, sitting down. "Then what on Human Earth made you act *Midsummer Night's Dream* three times over, *on* Midsummer Eve, *in* the middle of a Ring, and under – right *under* one of my oldest hills in Old England? Pook's Hill – Puck's Hill – Puck's Hill – Pook's Hill! It's as plain as the nose on my face."

He pointed to the bare, fern-covered slope of Pook's Hill that runs up from the far side of the mill-stream to a dark wood. Beyond that wood the ground rises and rises for five

hundred feet, till at last you climb out on the bare top of
Beacon Hill, to look over the Pevensey Levels and the
Channel and half the naked South Downs.

"By Oak, Ash, and Thorn!" he cried, still laughing. "If
this had happened a few hundred years ago you'd have had
all the People of the Hills out like bees in June!"

"We didn't know it was wrong," said Dan.

"Wrong!" The little fellow shook with laughter. "Indeed,
it isn't wrong. You've done something that Kings and
Knights and Scholars in old days would have given their
crowns and spurs and books to find out. If Merlin himself
had helped you, you couldn't have managed better! You've
broken the Hills – you've broken the Hills! It hasn't happened in a thousand years."

"We – we didn't mean to," said Una.

"Of course you didn't! That's just why you did it. Un-
luckily the Hills are empty now, and all the People of the
Hills are gone. I'm the only one left. I'm Puck, the oldest
Old Thing in England, very much at your service if – if you
care to have anything to do with me. If you don't, of course
you've only to say so, and I'll go."

He looked at the children, and the children looked at him
for quite half a minute. His eyes did not twinkle any more.
They were very kind, and there was the beginning of a good
smile on his lips.

Una put out her hand. "Don't go," she said. "We like you."

"Have a Bath Oliver," said Dan, and he passed over the
squashy envelope with the eggs.

"By Oak, Ash and Thorn," cried Puck, taking off his blue
cap, "I like you too. Sprinkle a plenty salt on the biscuit,
Dan, and I'll eat it with you. That'll show you the sort of
person *I* am. Some of us" – he went on, with his mouth
full – "couldn't abide Salt, or Horse-shoes over a door, or
Mountain-ash berries, or Running Water, or Cold Iron, or
the sound of Church Bells. But I'm Puck!"

He brushed the crumbs carefully from his doublet and shook hands.

"We always said, Dan and I," Una stammered, "that if it ever happened we'd know exactly what to do; but – but now it seems all different somehow."

"She means meeting a fairy," said Dan. "*I* never believed in 'em – not after I was six, anyhow."

"I did," said Una. "At least, I sort of half believed till we learned 'Farewell, Rewards'. Do you know 'Farewell, Rewards and Fairies'?"

"Do you mean this?" said Puck. He threw his big head back and began at the second line:

> "Good housewives now may say,
> For now foul sluts in dairies
> Do fare as well as they;
> And though they sweep their hearths no less,

("Join in, Una!")

> Than maids were wont to do,
> Yet who of late for cleanliness
> Finds sixpence in her shoe?"

The echoes flapped all along the flat meadow.

"Of course I know it," he said.

"And then there's the verse about the Rings," said Dan. "When I was little it always made me feel unhappy in my inside."

" 'Witness those rings and roundelays', do you mean?" boomed Puck, with a voice like a great church organ.

> "Of theirs which yet remain,
> Were footed in Queen Mary's days
> On many a grassy plain,
> But since of late Elizabeth,

And, later, James came in,
Are never seen on any heath
As when the time hath been."

"It's some time since I heard that sung, but there's no good beating about the bush: it's true. The People of the Hills have all left. I saw them come into Old England and I saw them go. Giants, trolls, kelpies, brownies, goblins, imps; wood, tree, mound, and water spirits; heath-people, hill-watchers, treasure-guards, good people, little people, pishogues, leprechauns, night-riders, pixies, nixies, gnomes, and the rest – gone, all gone! I came into England with Oak, Ash and Thorn, and when Oak, Ash and Thorn are gone I shall go too."

Dan looked round the meadow – at Una's Oak by the lower gate; at the line of ash trees that overhang Otter Pool where the mill-stream spills over when the Mill does not need it, and at the gnarled old white-thorn where Three Cows scratched their necks.

"It's all right," he said; and added, "I'm planting a lot of acorns this autumn too."

"Then aren't you most awfully old?" said Una.

"Not old – fairly long-lived, as folk say hereabouts. Let me see – my friends used to set my dish of cream for me o' nights when Stonehenge was new. Yes, before the Flint Men made the Dewpond under Chanctonbury Ring."

Una clasped her hands, cried "Oh!" and nodded her head.

"She's thought a plan," Dan explained. "She always does like that when she thinks a plan."

"I was thinking – suppose we saved some of our porridge and put it in the attic for you? They'd notice if we left it in the nursery."

"Schoolroom," said Dan quickly, and Una flushed, because they had made a solemn treaty that summer not to call the schoolroom the nursery any more.

"Bless your heart o' gold!" said Puck. "You'll make a fine considering wench some market-day. I really don't want you to put out a bowl for me; but if ever I need a bite, be sure I'll tell you."

He stretched himself at length on the dry grass, and the children stretched out beside him, their bare legs waving happily in the air. They felt they could not be afraid of him any more than of their particular friend old Hobden the hedger. He did not bother them with grown-up questions, or laugh at the donkey's head, but lay and smiled to himself in the most sensible way.

"Have you a knife on you?" he said at last.

Dan handed over his big one-bladed outdoor knife, and Puck began to carve out a piece of turf from the centre of the Ring.

"What's that for – Magic?" said Una, as he pressed up the square of chocolate loam that cut like so much cheese.

"One of my little magics," he answered, and cut another. "You see, I can't let you into the Hills because the People of the Hills have gone; but if you care to take seisin from me, I may be able to show you something out of the common here on Human Earth. You certainly deserve it."

"What's taking seisin?" said Dan, cautiously.

"It's an old custom the people had when they bought and sold land. They used to cut out a clod and hand it over to the buyer, and you weren't lawfully seised of your land – it didn't really belong to you – till the other fellow had actually given you a piece of it – like this." He held out the turves.

"But it's our own meadow," said Dan, drawing back. "Are you going to magic it away?"

Puck laughed. "I know it's your meadow, but there's a great deal more in it than you or your father ever guessed. Try!"

He turned his eyes on Una.

"I'll do it," she said. Dan followed her example at once.

"Now are you two lawfully seised and possessed of all Old England," began Puck, in a sing-song voice. "By right of Oak, Ash and Thorn are you free to come and go and look and know where I shall show or best you please. You shall see What you shall see and you shall hear What you shall hear, though It shall have happened three thousand year; and you shall know neither Doubt nor Fear. Fast! Hold fast all I give you."

The children shut their eyes, but nothing happened.

"Well?" said Una, disappointedly opening them. "I thought there would be dragons."

"Though It shall have happened three thousand year," said Puck, and counted on his fingers. "No; I'm afraid there were no dragons three thousand years ago."

"But there hasn't happened anything at all," said Dan.

"Wait awhile," said Puck. "You don't grow an oak in a year – and Old England's older than twenty oaks. Let's sit down again and think. *I* can do that for a century at a time."

"Ah, but you're a fairy," said Dan.

"Have you ever heard me say that word yet?" said Puck quickly.

"No. You talk about 'the People of the Hills', but you never say 'fairies'," said Una. "I was wondering at that. Don't you like it?"

"How would you like to be called 'mortal' or 'human being' all the time," said Puck; "or 'son of Adam' or 'daughter of Eve'?"

"I shouldn't like it at all," said Dan. "That's how the Djinns and Afrits talk in the *Arabian Nights.*"

"And that's how I feel about saying – that word that I don't say. Besides, what you call *them* are made-up things the People of the Hills have never heard of – little buzzflies with butterfly wings and gauze petticoats, and shiny stars in their hair, and a wand like a schoolteacher's cane for punishing bad boys and rewarding good ones. I know 'em!"

"We don't mean that sort," said Dan. "We hate 'em too."

"Exactly," said Puck. "Can you wonder that the People of the Hills don't care to be confused with that painty-winged, wand-waving, sugar-and-shake-your-head set of impostors? Butterfly wings, indeed! I've seen Sir Huon and a troop of his people setting off from Tintagel Castle for Hy-Brasil in the teeth of a sou'-westerly gale, with the spray flying all over the Castle, and the Horses of the Hills wild with fright. Out they'd go in a lull, screaming like gulls, and back they'd be driven five good miles inland before they could ·come head to wind again. Butterfly-wings! It was Magic – Magic as black as Merlin could make it, and the whole sea was green fire and white foam with singing mermaids in it. And the Horses of the Hills picked their way from one wave to another by the lightning flashes! *That* was how it was in the old days!"

"Splendid," said Dan, but Una shuddered.

"I'm glad they're gone, then; but what made the People of the Hills go away?" Una asked.

"Different things. I'll tell you one of them some day the thing that made the biggest flit of any," said Puck. "But they didn't all flit at once. They dropped off, one by one, through the centuries. Most of them were foreigners who couldn't stand our climate. *They* flitted early."

"How early?" said Dan.

"A couple of thousand years or more. The fact is they began as Gods. The Phoenicians brought some over when they came to buy tin; and the Gauls, and the Jutes, and the Danes, and the Frisians, and the Angles brought more when they landed. They were always landing in those days, or being driven back to their ships, and they always brought their Gods with them. England is a bad country for Gods. Now, *I* began as I mean to go on. A bowl of porridge, a dish of milk, and a little quiet fun with the country folk in the lanes was enough for me then, as it is now. I belong here, you see, and I have been mixed up with people all my days. But most of the others insisted on being Gods, and having temples, and altars, and priests, and sacrifices of their own."

"People burned in wicker baskets?" said Dan. "Like Miss Blake tells us about?"

"All sorts of sacrifices," said Puck. "If it wasn't men, it was horses, or cattle, or pigs, or metheglin – that's a sticky, sweet sort of beer. *I* never liked it. They were a stiff-necked, extravagant set of idols, the Old Things. But what was the result? Men don't like being sacrificed at the best of times; they don't even like sacrificing their farm-horses. After a while, men simply left the Old Things alone, and the roofs of their temples fell in, and the Old Things had to scuttle out and pick up a living as they could. Some of them took to hanging about trees, and hiding in graves and groaning o' nights. If they groaned loud enough and long enough they might frighten a poor countryman into sacrificing a hen, or leaving a pound of butter for them. I remember one Goddess called Belisama. She became a common wet water-spirit somewhere in Lancashire. And there were hundreds of other friends of mine. First they were Gods. Then they were People of the Hills, and then they flitted to other places because they couldn't get on with the English for one reason or another. There was only one Old Thing, I remember, who honestly worked for his living after he came down in the world. He was called Weland, and he was a smith to some Gods. I've forgotten their names, but he used to make them swords and spears. I think he claimed kin with Thor of the Scandinavians."

"*Heroes of Asgard* Thor?" said Una. She had been reading the book.

"Perhaps," answered Puck. "None the less, when bad

times came, he didn't beg or steal. He worked; and I was lucky enough to be able to do him a good turn."

"Tell us about it," said Dan. "I think I like hearing of Old Things."

They rearranged themselves comfortably, each chewing a grass stem. Puck propped himself on one strong arm and went on:

"Let's think! I met Weland first on a November afternoon in a sleet storm, on Pevensey Level –"

"Pevensey? Over the hill, you mean?" Dan pointed south.

"Yes; but it was all marsh in those days, right up to Horsebridge and Hydeneye. I was on Beacon Hill – they called it Brunanburgh then – when I saw the pale flame that burning thatch makes, and I went down to look. Some pirates – I think they must have been Peofn's men were burning a village on the Levels, and Weland's image – a big, black wooden thing with amber beads round his neck – lay in the bows of a black thirty-two-oar galley that they had just beached. Bitter cold it was! There were icicles hanging from her deck and the oars were glazed over with ice, and there was ice on Weland's lips. When he saw me he began a long chant in his own tongue, telling me how he was going to rule England, and how I should smell the smoke of his altars from Lincolnshire to the Isle of Wight. *I* didn't care! I'd seen too many Gods charging into Old England to be upset about it. I let him sing himself out while his men were burning the village, and then I said (I don't know what put it into my head), 'Smith of the Gods,' I said, 'the time comes when I shall meet you plying your trade for hire by the wayside.'"

"What did Weland say?" said Una. "Was he angry?"

"He called me names and rolled his eyes, and I went away to wake up the people inland. But the pirates conquered the country, and for centuries Weland was a most important God. He had temples everywhere – from Lincolnshire to the Isle of Wight, as he said – and his sacrifices were simply scandalous. To do him justice, he preferred horses to men; but men *or* horses, I knew that presently he'd have to come down in the world – like the other Old Things. I gave him lots of time – I gave him about a thousand years – and at the end of 'em I went into one of his temples near Andover to see how he prospered. There was his altar, and there was his image, and there were his priests, and there were the congregation, and everybody seemed quite happy, except Weland and the priests. In the old days the congregation were unhappy until the priests had chosen their sacrifices; and so would *you* have been. When the service began a priest rushed out, dragged a man up to the altar, pretended to hit him on the head with a little gilt axe, and the man fell down and pretended to die. Then everybody shouted: 'A sacrifice to Weland! A sacrifice to Weland!'"

"And the man wasn't really dead?" said Una.

"Not a bit. All as much pretence as a dolls' tea-party. Then they brought out a splendid white horse, and the priest cut some hair from its mane and tail and burned it on the altar, shouting, 'A sacrifice!' That counted the same as if a man and a horse had been killed. I saw poor Weland's face through the smoke, and I couldn't help laughing. He looked so disgusted and so hungry, and all he had to satisfy himself was a horrid smell of burning hair. Just a dolls' tea-party!"

"I judged it better not to say anything then ('twouldn't have been fair), and the next time I came to Andover, a few hundred years later, Weland and his temple were gone, and there was a Christian bishop in a church there. None of the People of the Hills could tell me anything about him, and I supposed that he had left England." Puck turned, lay on his other elbow, and thought for a long time.

"Let's see," he said at last. "It must have been some few years later – a year or two before the Conquest, I think— that I came back to Pook's Hill here, and one evening I heard old Hobden talking about Weland's Ford."

"If you mean old Hobden the hedger, he's only seventy-two. He told me so himself," said Dan. "He's an intimate friend of ours."

"You're quite right," Puck replied. "I meant old Hobden's ninth great-grandfather. He was a free man and burned charcoal hereabouts. I've known the family, father and son, so long that I get confused sometimes. Hob of the Dene was my Hobden's name, and he lived at the Forge cottage. Of course, I pricked up my ears when I heard Weland mentioned, and I scuttled through the woods to the Ford just beyond Bog Wood yonder." He jerked his head westward, where the valley narrows between wooded hills and steep hop-fields.

"Why, that's Willingford Bridge," said Una. "We go there for walks often. There's a kingfisher there."

"It was Weland's Ford then, dearie. A road led down to it from the Beacon on the top of the hill – a shocking bad road it was – and all the hillside was thick, thick oak forest, with deer in it. There was no trace of Weland, but presently I saw a fat old farmer riding down from the Beacon under the greenwood tree. His horse had cast a shoe in the clay, and when he came to the Ford he dismounted, took a penny out of his purse, laid it on a stone, tied the old horse to an oak, and called out: "Smith, Smith, here is work for you!" Then he sat down and went to sleep. You can imagine how *I* felt when I saw a white-bearded, bent old blacksmith in a leather apron creep out from behind the oak and begin to shoe the horse. It was Weland himself. I was so astonished that I jumped out and said: 'What on Human Earth are you doing here, Weland?'"

"Poor Weland!" sighed Una.

"He pushed the long hair back from his forehead (he didn't recognize me at first). Then he said: '*You* ought to know. You foretold it, Old Thing. I'm shoeing horses for hire. I'm not even Weland now,' he said. 'They call me Wayland-Smith.'"

"Poor chap!" said Dan. "What did you say?"

"What could I say? He looked up, with the horse's foot on his lap, and he said, smiling, 'I remember the time when I wouldn't have accepted this old bag of bones as a sacrifice, and now I'm glad enough to shoe him for a penny.'

'Isn't there any way for you to get back to Valhalla, or wherever you come from?' I said.

'I'm afraid not,' he said, rasping away at the hoof. He had a wonderful touch with horses. The old beast was whinnying on his shoulder. 'You may remember that I was not a gentle God in my Day and my Time and my Power. I shall never be released till some human being truly wishes me well.'

'Surely,' said I, 'the farmer can't do less than that. You're shoeing the horse all round for him.'

'Yes,' said he, 'and my nails will hold a shoe from one full moon to the next. But farmers and Weald clay,' said he, 'are both uncommon cold and sour.'

'Would you believe it, that when that farmer woke and found his horse shod he rode away without one word of thanks? I was so angry that I wheeled his horse right round and walked him back three miles to the Beacon, just to teach the old sinner politeness.'

"Were you invisible?" said Una. Puck nodded, gravely.

"The Beacon was always laid in those days ready to light, in case the French landed at Pevensey; and I walked the horse about and about it that lee-long summer night. The farmer thought he was bewitched – well, he *was*, of course – and began to pray and shout. *I* didn't care! I was as good a Christian as he any fair day in the County, and about four o'clock in the morning a young novice came along from the monastery that used to stand on the top of Beacon Hill."

"What's a novice?" said Dan.

"It really means a man who is beginning to be a monk, but in those days people sent their sons to a monastery just the same as a school. This young fellow had been to a monastery in France for a few months every year, and he was finishing his studies in the monastery close to his home here. Hugh was his name, and he had got up to go fishing hereabouts. His people owned all this valley. Hugh heard the farmer shouting, and asked him what in the world he meant. The old man spun him a wonderful tale about fairies and goblins and witches; and *I know* he hadn't seen a thing except rabbits and red deer all that night. (The People of the Hills are like otters – they don't show except when they choose.) But the novice wasn't a fool. He looked down at the horse's feet, and saw the new shoes fastened as only Weland knew how to fasten 'em. (Weland had a way of turning down the nails that folks called the Smith's Clinch.)

'H'm!' said the novice. 'Where did you get your horse shod?'

"The farmer wouldn't tell him at first, because the priests never liked their people to have any dealings with the Old Things. At last he confessed that the Smith had done it. 'What did you pay him?' said the novice. 'Penny,' said the farmer, very sulkily. 'That's less than a Christian would have charged,' said the novice. 'I hope you threw a "thank you" into the bargain.' 'No,' said the farmer; 'Wayland-Smith's a heathen.' 'Heathen or no heathen,' said the novice, 'you took his help, and where you get help there you must give thanks.' 'What?' said the farmer – he was in a furious temper because I was walking the old horse in circles all this time – 'What, you young jackanapes?' said he. 'Then by your reasoning I ought to say "Thank you" to Satan if he helped me?' 'Don't roll about up there splitting reasons with me,' said the novice. 'Come back to the Ford and thank the Smith, or you'll be sorry.'

"Back the farrner had to go. I led the horse, though no one saw me, and the novice walked beside us, his gown swishing through the shiny dew and his fishing-rod across his shoulders, spear-wise. When we reached the Ford again – it was five o'clock and misty still under the oaks – the farmer simply wouldn't say 'Thank you.' He said he'd tell the Abbot that the novice wanted him to worship heathen Gods. Then Hugh the novice lost his temper. He just cried, 'Out!' put his arm under the farmer's fat leg, and heaved him from his saddle on to the turf, and before he could rise he caught him by the back of the neck and shook him like a rat till the farmer growled, "Thank you, Wayland-Smith."

"Did Weland see all this?" said Dan.

"Oh yes, and he shouted his old war-cry when the farmer thudded on to the ground. He was delighted. Then the novice turned to the oak tree and said, 'Ho, Smith of the Gods! I am ashamed of this rude farmer; but for all you have done in kindness and charity to him and to others of our people, I thank you and wish you well.' Then he picked up his fishing-rod – it looked more like a tall spear than ever – and tramped off down your valley."

"And what did poor Weland do?" said Una.

"He laughed and he cried with joy, because he had been released at last, and could go away. But he was an honest Old Thing. He had worked for his living and he paid his debts before he left. 'I shall give that novice a gift,' said Weland. 'A gift that shall do him good the wide world over and Old England after him. Blow up my fire, Old Thing, while I get the iron for my last task.' Then he made a sword – a dark-grey, wavy-lined sword – and I blew the fire while he hammered. By Oak, Ash and Thorn, I tell you, Weland was a Smith of the Gods! He cooled that sword in running water twice, and the third time he cooled it in the evening dew; and he laid it out in the moonlight and said Runes (that's charms) over it, and he carved Runes of Prophecy on the blade. 'Old Thing,' he said to me, wiping his forehead, 'this is the best blade that Weland ever made. Even the user will never know how good it is. Come to the monastery.'

"We went to the dormitory where the monks slept, we saw the novice fast asleep in his cot, and Weland put the sword into his hand, and I remember the young fellow gripped it in his sleep. Then Weland strode as far as he dared into the Chapel and threw down all his shoeing-tools – his hammers and pincers and rasps – to show that he had done with them for ever. It sounded like suits of armour falling, and the sleepy monks ran in, for they thought the monastery had been attacked by the French. The novice came first of all, waving his new sword and shouting Saxon battle-cries. When they saw the shoeing-tools they were very bewildered, till the novice asked leave to speak, and told what he had done to the farmer, and what he had said to Wayland-Smith, and how, though the dormitory light was burning, he had found the wonderful Rune-carved sword in his cot.

"The Abbot shook his head at first, and then he laughed and said to the novice: 'Son Hugh, it needed no sign from a heathen God to show me that you will never be a monk. Take your sword, and keep your sword, and go with your sword, and be as gentle as you are strong and courteous. We will hang up the Smith's tools before the Altar,' he said, 'because, whatever the Smith of the Gods may have been in the old days, we know that he worked honestly for his living and made gifts to Mother Church.' Then they went to bed again, all except the novice, and he sat up in the garth playing with his sword. Then Weland said to me by the stables: 'Farewell, Old Thing; you had the right of it. You saw me come to England, and you see me go. Farewell!'

"With that he strode down the hill to the corner of the Great Woods – Woods Corner, you call it now – to the very place where he had first landed – and I heard him moving through the thickets towards Horsebridge for a little, and then he was gone. That was how it happened. I saw it."

Both children drew a long breath.

"But what happened to Hugh the novice?" said Una.

"And the sword?" said Dan.

Puck looked down the meadow that lay all quiet and cool in the shadow of Pook's Hill. A corncrake jarred in a hay-field near by, and the small trouts of the brook began to jump. A big white moth flew unsteadily from the alders and flapped round the children's heads, and the least little haze of water-mist rose from the brook.

"Do you really want to know?" Puck said.

"We do," cried the children. "Awfully!"

"Very good. I promised you that you shall see What you shall see, and you shall hear What you shall hear, though It shall have happened three thousand year; but just now it seems to me that, unless you go back to the house, people will be looking for you. I'll walk with you as far as the gate."

"Will you be here when we come again?" they asked.

"Surely, sure-ly," said Puck. "I've been here some time already. One minute first, please."

He gave them each three leaves – one of Oak, one of Ash and one of Thorn.

"Bite these," said he. "Otherwise you might be talking at home of what you've seen and heard, and – if I know human beings – they'd send for the doctor. Bite!"

They bit hard, and found themselves walking side by side to the lower gate. Their father was leaning over it.

"And how did your play go?" he asked.

"Oh, splendidly," said Dan. "Only afterwards, I think, we went to sleep. It was very hot and quiet. Don't you remember, Una?"

Una shook her head and said nothing.

"I see," said her father.

> "Late – late in the evening Kilmeny came home,
> For Kilmeny had been she could not tell where,
> And Kilmeny had seen what she could not declare.

But why are you chewing leaves at your time of life, daughter? For fun?"

"No. It was for something, but I can't exactly remember," said Una.

And neither of them could till –

A TREE SONG

> *Of all the trees that grow so fair,*
> *Old England to adorn,*
> *Greater are none beneath the Sun,*
> *Than Oak and Ash and Thorn.*
> *Sing Oak and Ash and Thorn, good Sirs*
> *(All of a Midsummer morn)!*
> *Surely we sing no little thing,*
> *In Oak and Ash and Thorn!*
>
> *Oak of the Clay lived many a day,*
> *Or ever Aeneas began;*
> *Ash of the Loam was a lady at home,*
> *When Brut was an outlaw man;*
> *Thorn of the Down saw New Troy Town*
> *(From which was London born);*
> *Witness hereby the ancientry*
> *Of Oak and Ash and Thorn!*

Yew that is old in churchyard mould,
  He breedeth a mighty bow;
Alder for shoes do wise men choose,
  And beech for cups also.
But when ye have killed, and your bowl is spilled,
  And your shoes are clean outworn,
Back ye must speed for all that ye need,
  To Oak and Ash and Thorn!

Ellum she hateth mankind, and waiteth
  Till every gust be laid,
To drop a limb on the head of him
  That anyway trusts her shade:
But whether a lad be sober or sad,
  Or mellow with ale from the horn,
He will take no wrong when he lieth along
  'Neath Oak and Ash and Thorn!

Oh, do not tell the Priest our plight,
  Or he would call it a sin;
But – we have been out in the woods all night,
  A-conjuring Summer in!
And we bring you news by word of mouth –
  Good news for cattle and corn –
Now is the Sun come up from the South,
  With Oak and Ash and Thorn!

Sing Oak and Ash and Thorn, good Sirs
  (All of a Midsummer morn)!
England shall bide till Judgment Tide,
  By Oak and Ash and Thorn!

Young Men at the Manor

They were fishing, a few days later, in the bed of the brook that for centuries had cut deep into the soft valley soil. The trees closing overhead made long tunnels through which the sunshine worked in blobs and patches. Down in the tunnels were bars of sand and gravel, old roots and trunks covered with moss or painted red by the irony water; foxgloves growing lean and pale towards the light; clumps of fern and thirsty shy flowers who could not live away from moisture and shade. In the pools you could see the wave thrown up by the trouts as they charged hither and yon, and the pools were joined to each other – except in flood-time, when all was one brown rush – by sheets of thin broken water that poured themselves chuckling round the darkness of the next bend.

This was one of the children's most secret hunting-grounds, and their particular friend, old Hobden the hedger, had shown them how to use it. Except for the click of a rod hitting a low willow, or a switch and tussle among the young ash leaves as a line hung up for the minute, nobody in the hot pasture could have guessed what game was going on among the trouts below the banks.

"We've got half a dozen," said Dan, after a warm, wet hour. "I vote we go up to Stone Bay and try Long Pool."

Una nodded – most of her talk was by nods – and they crept from the gloom of the tunnels towards the tiny weir that turns the brook into the mill-stream. Here the banks are low and bare, and the glare of the afternoon sun on the Long Pool below the weir makes your eyes ache.

When they were in the open they nearly fell down with

astonishment. A huge grey horse, whose tail hairs crinkled the glassy water, was drinking in the pool, and the ripples about his muzzle flashed like melted gold. On his back sat an old, white-haired man dressed in a loose glimmery gown of chain-mail. He was bare-headed, and a nut-shaped iron helmet hung at his saddle bow. His reins were of red leather five or six inches deep, scalloped at the edges, and his high padded saddle with its red girths was held fore and aft by a red leather breastband and crupper.

"Look!" said Una, as though Dan were not staring his very eyes out. "It's like the picture in your room – 'Sir Isumbras at the Ford'."

The rider turned towards them, and his thin, long face was just as sweet and gentle as that of the knight who carries the children in that picture.

"They should be here now, Sir Richard," said Puck's deep voice among the willow-herb.

"They are here," the knight said, and he smiled at Dan with the string of trouts in his hand. "There seems no great change in boys since mine fished this water."

"If your horse has drunk, we shall be more at ease in the Ring," said Puck; and he nodded to the children as though he had never magicked away their memories a week before.

The great horse turned and hoisted himself into the pasture with a kick and a scramble that tore the clods down rattling.

"Your pardon!" said Sir Richard to Dan. "When these lands were mine, I never loved that mounted men should cross the brook except by the paved ford. But my Swallow here was thirsty, and I wished to meet you."

"We're very glad you've come, sir," said Dan. "It doesn't matter in the least about the banks."

He trotted across the pasture on the sword side of the mighty horse, and it was a mighty iron-handled sword that swung from Sir Richard's belt. Una walked behind with Puck. She remembered everything now.

"I'm sorry about the Leaves," he said, "but it would never have done if you had gone home and told, would it?"

"I s'pose not," Una answered. "But you said that all the fair – People of the Hills had left England."

"So they have; but I told you that you should come and go and look and know, didn't I? The knight isn't a fairy. He's Sir Richard Dalyngridge, a very old friend of mine. He came over with William the Conqueror, and he wants to see you particularly."

"What for?" said Una.

"On account of your great wisdom and learning," Puck replied, without a twinkle.

"Us?" said Una. "Why, I don't know my Nine Times not to say it dodging, and Dan makes the most *awful* mess of fractions. He can't mean *us* !"

"Una!" Dan called back. "Sir Richard says he is going to tell what happened to Weland's sword. He's got it. Isn't it splendid?"

"Nay – nay," said Sir Richard, dismounting as they reached the Ring, in the bend of the mill-stream bank. "It is you that must tell me, for I hear the youngest child in our England today is as wise as our wisest clerk." He slipped the bit out of Swallow's mouth, dropped the ruby-red reins over his head, and the wise horse moved off to graze.

Sir Richard (they noticed he limped a little) unslung his great sword.

"That's it," Dan whispered to Una.

"This is the sword that Brother Hugh had from Wayland-Smith," Sir Richard said. "Once he gave it me, but I would not take it; but at the last it became mine after such a fight as never christened man fought. See!" He half drew it from its sheath and turned it before them. On either side just be-low the handle, where the Runic letters shivered as though they were alive, were two deep gouges in the dull, deadly steel. "Now, what Thing made those?" said he. "I know not, but you, perhaps, can say."

"Tell them all the tale, Sir Richard," said Puck. "It concerns their land somewhat."

"Yes, from the very beginning," Una pleaded, for the knight's good face and the smile on it more than ever reminded her of 'Sir Isumbras at the Ford'.

They settled down to listen, Sir Richard bare-headed to the sunshine, dandling the sword in both hands, while the grey horse cropped outside the Ring, and the helmet on the saddle-bow clinged softly each time he jerked his head.

"From the beginning, then," Sir Richard said, "since it concerns your land, I will tell the tale. When our Duke came out of Normandy to take his England, great knights (have ye heard?) came and strove hard to serve the Duke, because he promised them lands here, and small knights followed the great ones. My folk in Normandy were poor; but a great knight, Engerrard of the Eagle – Engenulf De Aquila – who was kin to my father, followed the Earl of Mortain, who followed William the Duke, and I followed De Aquila. Yes, with thirty men-at-arms out of my father's house and a new sword, I set out to conquer England three days after I was made knight. I did not then know that England would conquer me. We went up to Santlache with the rest – a very great host of us."

"Does that mean the Battle of Hastings – Ten Sixty-Six?" Una whispered, and Puck nodded, so as not to interrupt.

"At Santlache, over the hill yonder" – he pointed southeastward towards Fairlight – "we found Harold's men. We fought. At the day's end they ran. My men went with De Aquila's to chase and plunder, and in that chase Engerrard of the Eagle was slain, and his son Gilbert took his banner and his men forward. This I did not know till after, for

Swallow here was cut in the flank, so I stayed to wash the wound at a brook by a thorn. There a single Saxon cried out to me in French, and we fought together. I should have known his voice, but we fought together. For a long time neither had any advantage, till by pure ill-fortune his foot slipped and his sword flew from his hand. Now I had but newly been made knight, and wished, above all, to be courteous and fameworthy, so I forbore to strike and bade him get his sword again. 'A plague on my sword,' said he. 'It has lost me my first fight. You have spared my life. Take my sword.' He held it out to me, but as I stretched my hand the sword groaned like a stricken man, and I leaped back crying, 'Sorcery!'

(The children looked at the sword as though it might speak again.)

"Suddenly a clump of Saxons ran out upon me and, seeing a Norman alone, would have killed me, but my Saxon cried out that I was his prisoner, and beat them off. Thus, see you, he saved my life. He put me on my horse and led me through the woods ten long miles to this valley."

"To here, d'you mean?" said Una.

"To this very valley. We came in by the Lower Ford under the King's Hill yonder" – he pointed eastward where the valley widens.

"And was that Saxon Hugh the novice?" Dan asked.

"Yes, and more than that. He had been for three years at the monastery at Bec by Rouen, where" – Sir Richard chuckled – "the Abbot Herluin would not suffer me to remain."

"Why wouldn't he?" said Dan.

"Because I rode my horse into the refectory, when the scholars were at meat, to show the Saxon boys we Normans were not afraid of an Abbot. It was that very Saxon Hugh tempted me to do it, and we had not met since that day. I thought I knew his voice even inside my helmet, and, for all that our Lords fought, we each rejoiced we had not slain the other. He walked by my side, and he told me how a heathen God, as he believed, had given him his sword, but he said he had never heard it sing before. I remember I warned him to beware of sorcery and quick enchantments. Sir Richard smiled to himself. "I was very young – very young!"

"When we came to his house here we had almost forgotten that we had been at blows. It was near midnight, and the Great Hall was full of men and women waiting news. There I first saw his sister, the Lady Aelueva, of whom he had spoken to us in France. She cried out fiercely at me, and would have had me hanged in that hour, but her brother said that I had spared his life – he said not how he saved mine from the Saxons – and that our Duke had won the day; and even while they wrangled over my poor body, of a sudden he fell down in a swoon from his wounds.

"'This is *thy* fault,' said the Lady Aelueva to me, and she kneeled above him and called for wine and cloths.

"'If I had known,' I answered, 'he should have ridden and I walked. But he set me on my horse; he made no complaint; he walked beside me and spoke merrily throughout. I pray I have done him no harm.'

"'Thou hast need to pray,' she said, catching up her underlip. 'If he dies, thou shalt hang.'

"They bore off Hugh to his chamber; but three tall men of the house bound and set me under the beam of the Great Hall with a rope round my neck. The end of the rope they flung over the beam, and they sat them down by the fire to wait word whether Hugh lived or died. They cracked nuts with their knife-hilts the while."

"And how did you feel?" said Dan.

"Very weary; but I did heartily pray for my schoolmate Hugh his health. About noon I heard horses in the valley, and the three men loosed my ropes and fled out, and De Aquila's men rode up. Gilbert de Aquila came with them, for it was his boast that, like his father, he forgot no man that served him. He was little, like his father, but terrible, with a nose like an eagle's nose and yellow eyes like an eagle. He rode tall warhorses – roans, which he bred himself – and he could never abide to be helped into the saddle. He saw the rope hanging from the beam and laughed, and his men laughed, for I was too stiff to rise.

"'This is poor entertainment for a Norman knight,' he said, 'but, such as it is, let us be grateful. Show me, boy, to whom thou owest most, and we will pay them out of hand.'

"What did he mean? To kill 'em?" said Dan.

"Assuredly. But I looked at the Lady Aeluerva where she stood among her maids, and her brother beside her. De Aquila's men had driven them all into the Great Hall."

"Was she pretty?" said Una.

"In all my long life I have never seen woman fit to strew rushes before my Lady Aeluerva," the knight replied, quite simply and quietly. "As I looked at her I thought I might save her and her house by a jest."

"'Seeing that I came somewhat hastily and without warning,' said I to De Aquila, 'I have no fault to find with the courtesy that these Saxons have shown me.' But my voice shook. It is – it was not good to jest with that little man.

"All were silent awhile, till De Aquila laughed. 'Look, men – a miracle,' said he. 'The fight is scarce sped, my father is not yet buried, and here we find our youngest knight already set down in his Manor, while his Saxons ye can see it in their fat faces – have paid him homage and service! By the Saints,' he said, rubbing his nose, 'I never thought England would be so easy won! Surely I can do no less than give the lad what he has taken. This Manor shall be thine, boy,' he said, 'till I come again, or till thou art slain. Now, mount, men, and ride. We follow our Duke into Kent to make him King of England.'

"He drew me with him to the door while they brought his

horse – a lean roan, taller than my Swallow here, but not so
well girthed.

"'Hark to me,' he said, fretting with his great war-gloves.
'I have given thee this Manor, which is a Saxon hornets'
nest, and I think thou wilt be slain in a month as my father
was slain. Yet if thou canst keep the roof on the hall, the
thatch on the barn, and the plough in the furrow till I come
back, thou shalt hold the Manor from me; for the Duke has
promised our Earl Mortain all the lands by Pevensey, and
Mortain will give me of them what he would have given my
father. God knows if thou or I shall live till England is won;
but remember, boy, that here and now fighting is foolishness and' – he reached for the reins – 'craft and cunning is
all.'

"'Alas, I have no cunning,' said I.

"'Not yet,' said he, hopping abroad, foot in stirrup, and
poking his horse in the belly with his toe. 'Not yet, but I
think thou hast a good teacher. Farewell! Hold the Manor
and live. Lose the Manor and hang,' he said, and spurred
out, his shield-straps squeaking behind him.

"So, children, here was I, little more than a boy, and
Santlache fight not two days old, left alone with my thirty
men-at-arms, in a land I knew not, among a people whose
tongue I could not speak, to hold down the land which I had
taken from them."

"And that was here at home?" said Una.

"Yes, here. See! From the Upper Ford, Weland's Ford, to
the Lower Ford, by the Belle Allée, west and east it ran half
a league. From the Beacon of Brunanburgh behind us here,
south and north it ran a full league – and all the woods were
full of broken men from Santlache, Saxon thieves, Norman
plunderers, robbers, and deer-stealers. A hornets' nest indeed!

"When De Aquila had gone, Hugh would have thanked
me for saving their lives; but the Lady Aelueva said that

I had done it only for the sake of receiving the Manor."

"'How could I know that De Aquila would give it me?' I said. 'If I had told him I had spent my night in your halter he would have burned the place twice over by now.'

"'If any man had put *my* neck in a rope,' she said, 'I would have seen his house burned thrice over before I would have made terms.'

"'But it was a woman,' I said; and I laughed, and she wept and said that I mocked her in her captivity.

"'Lady,' said I, 'there is no captive in this valley except one, and he is not a Saxon.'

"At this she cried that I was a Norman thief, who came with false, sweet words, having intended from the first to turn her out in the fields to beg her bread. Into the fields! She had never seen the face of war!

"I was angry, and answered, 'This much at least I can disprove, for I swear' – and on my sword-hilt I swore it in that place – 'I swear I will never set foot in the Great Hall till the Lady Aeluev herself shall summon me there.'

"She went away, saying nothing, and I walked out, and Hugh limped after me, whistling dolorously (that is a custom of the English), and we came upon the three Saxons that had bound me. They were now bound by my men-at-arms, and behind them stood some fifty stark and sullen churls of the House and the Manor, waiting to see what should fall. We heard De Aquila's trumpets blow thin through the woods Kentward.

"'Shall we hang these?' said my men.

"'Then my churls will fight,' said Hugh, beneath his breath; but I bade him ask the three what mercy they hoped for.

"'None,' said they all. 'She bade us hang thee if our master died. And we would have hanged thee. There is no more to it.'

"As I stood doubting, a woman ran down from the oak

wood above the King's Hill yonder, and cried out that some
Normans were driving off the swine there.

"'Norman or Saxon,' said I, 'we must beat them back, or
they will rob us every day. Out at them with any arms ye
have!' So I loosed those three carles and we ran together,
my men-at-arms and the Saxons with bills and axes which
they had hidden in the thatch of their huts, and Hugh led
them. Halfway up the King's Hill we found a false fellow
from Picardy – a sutler that sold wine in the Duke's camp –
with a dead knight's shield on his arm, a stolen horse under
him, and some ten or twelve wastrels at his tail, all cutting
and slashing at the pigs. We beat them off, and saved our
pork. One hundred and seventy pigs we saved in that great
battle." Sir Richard laughed.

"That, then, was our first work together, and I bade Hugh
tell his folk that so would I deal with any man, knight or
churl, Norman or Saxon, who stole as much as one egg
from our valley. Said he to me, riding home:

"'Thou hast gone far to conquer England this evening.' I
answered: 'England must be thine and mine, then. Help me,
Hugh, to deal aright with these people. Make them to know
that if they slay me De Aquila will surely send to slay them,
and he will put a worse man in my place.' 'That may well
be true,' said he, and gave me his hand. 'Better the devil we
know than the devil we know not, till we can pack you
Normans home.' And so, too, said his Saxons; and they
laughed as we drove the pigs downhill. But I think some of
them, even then, began not to hate me."

"I like Brother Hugh," said Una, softly.

"Beyond question he was the most perfect, courteous,
valiant, tender, and wise knight that ever drew breath," said
Sir Richard, caressing the sword. "He hung up his sword –
this sword – on the wall of the Great Hall, because he said it
was fairly mine, and never he took it down till De Aquila
returned, as I shall presently show. For three months his men

and mine guarded the valley, till all robbers and night-walkers learned there was nothing to get from us save hard tack and a hanging. Side by side we fought against all who came – thrice a week sometimes we fought – against thieves and landless knights looking for good manors. Then we were in some peace, and I made shift by Hugh's help to govern the valley – for all this valley of yours was my Manor – as a knight should. I kept the roof on the hall and the thatch on the barn, but . . . the English are a bold people. His Saxons would laugh and jest with Hugh, and Hugh with them, and – this was marvellous to me – if even the meanest of them said that such and such a thing was the Custom of the Manor, then straightway would Hugh and such old men of the Manor as might be near forsake everything else to debate the matter – I have seen them stop the Mill with the corn half ground – and if the custom or usage were proven to be as it was said, why, that was the end of it, even though it were flat against Hugh, his wish and command. Wonderful!"

"Aye," said Puck, breaking in for the first time. "The Custom of Old England was here before your Norman knights came, and it outlasted them, though they fought against it cruel."

"Not I," said Sir Richard. "I let the Saxons go their stubborn way, but when my own men-at-arms, Normans not six months in England, stood up and told me what was the custom of the country, *then* I was angry. Ah, good days! Ah, wonderful people! And I loved them all."

The knight lifted his arms as though he would hug the whole dear valley, and Swallow, hearing the chink of his chain mail, looked up and whinnied softly.

"At last," he went on, "after a year of striving and contriving and some little driving, De Aquila came to the valley, alone and without warning. I saw him first at the Lower Ford, with a swineherd's brat on his saddle-bow.

"'There is no need for thee to give any account of thy stewardship,' said he. 'I have it all from the child here.' And he told me how the young thing had stopped his tall horse at the Ford, by waving of a branch, and crying that the way was barred. 'And if one bold, bare babe be enough to guard the Ford in these days, thou hast done well,' said he, and puffed and wiped his head.

"He pinched the child's cheek, and looked at our cattle in the flat by the river.

"'Both fat,' said he, rubbing his nose. 'This is craft and cunning such as I love. What did I tell thee when I rode away, boy?'

"'Hold the Manor or hang' said I. I had never forgotten it. 'True. And thou hast held.' He clambered from his saddle and with his sword's point cut out a turf from the bank and gave it me where I kneeled."

Dan looked at Una, and Una looked at Dan.

"That's seisin," said Puck, in a whisper.

"'Now thou art lawfully seised of the Manor, Sir Richard,' said he – 'twas the first time he ever called me that – 'thou and thy heirs for ever. This must serve till the King's clerks write out thy title on a parchment. England is all ours – if we can hold it.'

"'What service shall I pay?' I asked, and I remember I was proud beyond words.

"'Knight's fee, boy, knight's fee!' said he, hopping round his horse on one foot. (Have I said he was little, and could not endure to be helped to his saddle?) 'Six mounted men or twelve archers thou shalt send me whenever I call for them, and – where got you that corn?' said he, for it was near harvest, and our corn stood well. 'I have never seen such bright straw. Send me three bags of the same seed yearly, and furthermore, in memory of our last meeting – with the rope round thy neck entertain me and my men for two days of each year in the Great Hall of thy Manor.'

"'Alas!' said I, 'then my Manor is already forfeit. I am under vow not to enter the Great Hall.' And I told him what I had sworn to the Lady Aelueva."

"And hadn't you ever been into the house since?" said Una.

"Never," Sir Richard answered, smiling. "I had made me a little hut of wood up the hill, and there I did justice and slept . . . De Aquila wheeled aside, and his shield shook on his back. 'No matter, boy,' said he. 'I will remit the homage for a year.'"

"He meant Sir Richard needn't give him dinner there the first year," Puck explained.

"De Aquila stayed with me in the hut, and Hugh, who could read and write and cast accounts, showed him the Roll of the Manor, in which were written all the names of our fields and men, and he asked a thousand questions touching the land, the timber, the grazing, the Mill, and the fish-ponds, and the worth of every man in the valley. But never he named the Lady Aelueva's name, nor went he near the Great Hall. By night he drank with us in the hut. Yes, he sat on the straw like an eagle ruffled in her feathers, his yellow eyes rolling above the cup, and he pounced in his talk like an eagle, swooping from one thing to another, but always binding fast. Yes; he would lie still awhile, and then rustle in the straw, and speak sometimes as though he were King William himself, and anon he would speak in parables and tales, and if at once we saw not his meaning he would yerk us in the ribs with his scabbarded sword.

"'Look you, boys,' said he, 'I am born out of my due time. Five hundred years ago I would have made all England such an England as neither Dane, Saxon, nor Norman should have conquered. Five hundred years hence I should have been such a counsellor to Kings as the world hath never dreamed of. 'Tis all here,' said he, tapping his big head, 'but it hath no play in this black age. Now Hugh here

is a better man than thou art, Richard.' He had made his
voice harsh and croaking, like a raven's.

"'Truth,' said I. 'But for Hugh, his help and patience and
long-suffering, I could never have kept the Manor.'

"'Nor thy life either,' said De Aquila. 'Hugh has saved
thee not once, but a hundred times. Be still, Hugh!' he said.
'Dost thou know, Richard, why Hugh slept, and why he still
sleeps, among thy Norman men-at-arms?'

"'To be near me,' said I, for I thought this was truth.

"'Fool!' said De Aquila. 'It is because his Saxons have
begged him to rise against thee, and to sweep every Norman out of the valley. No matter how I know. It is truth.
Therefore Hugh hath made himself an hostage for thy life,
well knowing that if any harm befell thee from his Saxons
thy Normans would slay him without remedy. And this his
Saxons know. Is it true, Hugh?'

"'In some sort,' said Hugh shamefacedly; 'at least, it was
true half a year ago. My Saxons would not harm Richard
now. I think they know him – but I judged it best to make
sure.'

"Look, children, what that man had done – and I had
never guessed it! Night after night had he lain down among
my men-at-arms, knowing that if one Saxon had lifted
knife against me, his life would have answered for mine.

"'Yes,' said De Aquila. 'And he is a swordless man.' He
pointed to Hugh's belt, for Hugh had put away his sword –
did I tell you? – the day after it flew from his hand at
Santlache. He carried only the short knife and the longbow.
'Swordless and landless art thou, Hugh; and they call thee
kin to Earl Godwin.' (Hugh was indeed of Godwin's
blood.) 'The Manor that was thine is given to this boy and
to his children for ever. Sit up and beg, for he can turn thee
out like a dog, Hugh.'

"Hugh said nothing, but I heard his teeth grind, and I
bade De Aquila, my own overlord, hold his peace, or I

would stuff his words down his throat. Then De Aquila laughed till the tears ran down his face.

"'I warned the King,' said he, 'what would come of giving England to us Norman thieves. Here art thou, Richard, less than two days confirmed in thy Manor, and already thou hast risen against thy overlord. What shall we do to him, *Sir* Hugh?'

"'I am a swordless man,' said Hugh. 'Do not jest with me,' and he laid his head on his knees and groaned.

"'The greater fool thou,' said De Aquila, and all his voice changed; 'for I have given thee the Manor of Dallington up the hill this half-hour since,' and he yerked at Hugh with his scabbard across the straw.

"'To me?' said Hugh. 'I am a Saxon, and, except that I love Richard here, I have not sworn fealty to any Norman.'

"'In God's good time, which because of my sins I shall not live to see, there will be neither Saxon nor Norman in England,' said De Aquila. 'If I know men, thou art more faithful unsworn than a score of Normans I could name. Take Dallington, and join Sir Richard to fight me tomorrow, if it please thee!'

"'Nay,' said Hugh. 'I am no child. Where I take a gift, there I render service'; and he put his hands between De Aquila's, and swore to be faithful, and, as I remember, I kissed him, and De Aquila kissed us both.

"We sat afterwards outside the hut while the sun rose, and De Aquila marked our churls going to their work in the fields, and talked of holy things, and how we should govern our Manors in time to come, and of hunting and of horse-breeding, and of the King's wisdom and unwisdom; for he spoke to us as though we were in all sorts now his brothers. Anon a churl stole up to me – he was one of the three I had not hanged a year ago – and he bellowed – which is the Saxon for whispering – that the Lady Aelueva would speak to me at the Great House. She walked abroad daily in the

Manor, and it was her custom to send me word whither she went, that I might set an archer or two behind and in front to guard her. Very often I myself lay up in the woods and watched on her also.

"I went swiftly, and as I passed the great door it opened from within, and there stood my Lady Aelueva, and she said to me: 'Sir Richard, will it please you enter your Great Hall?' Then she wept, but we were alone."

The knight was silent for a long time, his face turned across the valley, smiling.

"Oh, well done!" said Una, and clapped her hands very softly. "She was sorry, and she said so."

"Aye, she was sorry, and she said so," said Sir Richard, coming back with a little start. "Very soon – but *he* said it was two full hours later – De Aquila rode to the door, with his shield new scoured (Hugh had cleansed it), and demanded entertainment, and called me a false knight, that would starve his overlord to death. Then Hugh cried out that no man should work in the valley that day, and our Saxons blew horns, and set about feasting and drinking, and running of races, and dancing and singing; and De Aquila climbed upon a horse-block and spoke to them in what he swore was good Saxon, but no man understood it. At night we feasted in the Great Hall, and when the harpers and the singers were gone we four sat late at the high table. As I remember, it was a warm night with a full moon, and De Aquila bade Hugh take down his sword from the wall again, for the honour of the Manor of Dallington, and Hugh took it gladly enough. Dust lay on the hilt, for I saw him blow it off.

"She and I sat talking a little apart, and at first we thought the harpers had come back, for the Great Hall was filled with a rushing noise of music. De Aquila leaped up; but there was only the moonlight fretty on the floor.

"'Hearken!' said Hugh. 'It is my sword,' and as he belted it on, the music ceased.

"'Over Gods, forbid that I should ever belt blade like that,' said De Aquila. 'What does it foretell?'

"'The Gods that made it may know. Last time it spoke was at Hastings, when I lost all my lands. Belike it sings now that I have new lands and am a man again,' said Hugh.

"He loosed the blade a little and drove it back happily into the sheath, and the sword answered him low and crooningly, as – as a woman would speak to a man, her head on his shoulder.

"Now that was the second time in all my life I heard this Sword sing." . . .

"Look!" said Una. "There's Mother coming down the Long Slip. What will she say to Sir Richard? She can't help seeing him."

"And Puck can't magic us this time," said Dan.

"Are you sure?" said Puck; and he leaned forward and whispered to Sir Richard, who, smiling, bowed his head. – "But what befell the sword and my brother Hugh I will tell on another time," said he, rising. "Ohé, Swallow!"

The great horse cantered up from the far end of the meadow, close to Mother.

They heard Mother say: "Children, Gleason's old horse has broken into the meadow again. Where did he get through?"

"Just below Stone Bay," said Dan. "He tore down simple flobs of the bank! We noticed it just now. And we've caught no end of fish. We've been at it all the afternoon."

And they honestly believed that they had. They never noticed the Oak, Ash and Thorn leaves that Puck had slyly thrown into their laps.

Sir Richard's Song

I followed my Duke ere I was a lover,
*   To take from England fief and fee;*
But now this game is the other way over –
*   But now England hath taken me!*

I had my horse, my shield and banner,
*   And a boy's heart, so whole and free;*
But now I sing in another manner –
*   But now England hath taken me!*

As for my Father in his tower,
*   Asking news of my ship at sea;*
He will remember his own hour –
*   Tell him England hath taken me!*

As for my Mother in her bower,
*   That rules my Father so cunningly;*
She will remember a maiden's power –
*   Tell her England hath taken me!*

As for my Brother in Rouen city,
*   A nimble and naughty page is he;*
But he will come to suffer and pity –
*   Tell him England hath taken me!*

As for my little Sister waiting
*   In the pleasant orchards of Normandie;*
Tell her youth is the time of mating –
*   Tell her England hath taken me!*

As for my Comrades in camp and highway,
*   That lift their eyebrows scornfully;*
Tell them their way is not my way –
*   Tell them England hath taken me!*

Kings and Princes and Barons famèd,
*   Knights and Captains in your degree;*
Hear me a little before I am blamèd –
*   Seeing England hath taken me!*

Howso great man's strength be reckoned,
*   There are two things he cannot flee;*
Love is the first, and Death is the second –
*   And Love, in England, hath taken me!*

The Knights of the Joyous Venture

HARP SONG OF THE DANE WOMEN

What is a woman that you forsake her,
And the hearth-fire and the home-acre,
To go with the old grey Widow-maker?

She has no house to lay a guest in –
But one chill bed for all to rest in,
That the pale suns and the stray bergs nest in.

She has no strong white arms to fold you,
But the ten-times-fingering weed to hold you
Bound on the rocks where the tide has rolled you.

Yet, when the signs of summer thicken,
And the ice breaks, and the birch-buds quicken,
Yearly you turn from our side, and sicken –

Sicken again for the shouts and the slaughters, –
And steal away to the lapping waters,
And look at your ship in her winter quarters.

You forget our mirth, and talk at the tables,
The kine in the shed and the horse in the stables –
To pitch her sides and go over her cables!

Then you drive out where the storm-clouds swallow:
And the sound of your oar-blades falling hollow
Is all we have left through the months to follow.

Ah, what is Woman that you forsake her,
And the hearth-fire and the home-acre,
To go with the old grey Widow-maker?

It was too hot to run about in the open, so Dan asked their friend, old Hobden, to take their own dinghy from the pond and put her on the brook at the bottom of the garden. Her painted name was the *Daisy*, but for exploring expeditions she was the *Golden Hind* or the *Long Serpent,* or some such suitable name. Dan hiked and howked with a boat-hook (the brook was too narrow for sculls), and Una punted with a piece of hop-pole. When they came to a very shallow place (the *Golden Hind* drew quite three inches of water) they disembarked and scuffled her over the gravel by her tow-tope, and when they reached the overgrown banks beyond the garden they pulled themselves upstream by the low branches.

That day they intended to discover the North Cape like "Othere, the old sea-captain", in the book of verses which Una had brought with her; but on account of the heat they changed it to a voyage up the Amazon and the sources of the Nile. Even on the shaded water the air was hot and heavy with drowsy scents, while outside, through breaks in the trees, the sunshine burned the pasture like fire. The kingfisher was asleep on his watching-branch, and the blackbirds scarcely took the trouble to dive into the next bush. Dragonflies wheeling and clashing were the only things at work, except the moorhens and a big Red Admiral, who flapped down out of the sunshine for a drink.

When they reached Otter Pool the *Golden Hind* grounded comfortably on a shallow, and they lay beneath a roof of close green, watching the water trickle over the floodgates down the mossy brick chute from the mill-stream to the brook. A big trout – the children knew him well – rolled head and shoulders at some fly that sailed round the bend, while, once in just so often, the brook rose a fraction of an inch against all the wet pebbles, and they watched the slow draw and shiver of a breath of air through the tree-tops. Then the little voices of the slipping water began again.

"It's like the shadows talking, isn't it?" said Una. She had given up trying to read. Dan lay over the bows, trailing his hands in the current. They heard feet on the gravel-bar that runs half across the pool and saw Sir Richard Dalyngridge standing over them.

"Was yours a dangerous voyage?" he asked, smiling.

"She bumped a lot, sir," said Dan. "There's hardly any water this summer."

"Ah, the brook was deeper and wider when my children played at Danish pirates. Are you pirate-folk?"

"Oh no. We gave up being pirates years ago," explained Una. "We"re nearly always explorers now. Sailing round the world, you know."

"Round?" said Sir Richard. He sat him in the comfortable crotch of an old ash-root on the bank. "How can it be round?"

"Wasn't it in your books?" Dan suggested. He had been doing geography at his last lesson.

"I can neither write nor read," he replied. "Canst *thou* read, child?"

"Yes," said Dan, "barring the very long words."

"Wonderful! Read to me, that I may hear for myself."

Dan flushed, but opened the book and began gabbling a little – at "The Discoverer of the North Cape."

> "Othere, the old sea-captain,
>   Who dwelt in Helgoland,
> To King Alfred, the lover of truth,
> Brought a snow-white walrus-tooth,
>   Which he held in his brown right hand."

"But – but – this I know! This is an old song! This I have

heard sung! This is a miracle," Sir Richard interrupted.
"Nay, do not stop!" He leaned forward, and the shadows of
the leaves slipped and slid upon his chain-mail.

> " 'I ploughed the land with horses,
>   But my heart was ill at ease,
>   For the old seafaring men
>   Came to me now and then
>   With their sagas of the seas.' "

His hand fell on the hilt of the great sword. "This is
truth," he cried, "for so did it happen to me," and he beat
time delightedly to the tramp of verse after verse.

> " 'And now the land,' said Othere,
>   'Bent southward suddenly,
>   And I followed the curving shore,
>   And ever southward bore
>   Into a nameless sea.' "

"A nameless sea!" he repeated. "So did I – so did Hugh
and I."

"Where did you go? Tell us," said Una.

"Wait. Let me hear all first." So Dan read to the poem's
very end.

"Good," said the knight. "That is Othere's tale – even as I
have heard the men in the Dane ships sing it. Not in those
same valiant words, but something like to them."

"Have you ever explored North?" Dan shut the book.

"Nay. My venture was South. Farther South than any
man has fared, Hugh and I went down with Witta and his
heathen." He jerked the tall sword forward, and leaned on it
with both hands; but his eyes looked long past them.

"I thought you always lived here," said Una, timidly.

"Yes; while my Lady Aelueva lived. But she died. She

died. Then, my eldest son being a man, I asked De Aquila's leave that he should hold the Manor while I went on some journey or pilgrimage – to forget. De Aquila, whom the Second William had made Warden of Pevensey in Earl Mortain's place, was very old then, but still he rode his tall, roan horses, and in the saddle he looked like a little white falcon. When Hugh, at Dallington, over yonder, heard what I did, he sent for my second son, whom being unmarried he had ever looked upon as his own child, and, by De Aquila's leave, gave him the Manor of Dallington to hold till he should return. Then Hugh came with me."

"When did this happen?" said Dan.

"That I can answer to the very day, for as we rode with De Aquila by Pevensey – have I said that he was Lord of Pevensey and of the Honour of the Eagle? – to the Bordeaux ship that fetched him his wines yearly out of France, a Marsh man ran to us crying that he had seen a great black goat which bore on his back the body of the King, and that the goat had spoken to him. On that same day Red William our King, the Conqueror's son, died of a secret arrow while he hunted in a forest. "This is a cross matter," said De Aquila, "to meet on the threshold of a journey. If Red William be dead I may have to fight for my lands. Wait a little."

"My Lady being dead, I cared nothing for signs and omens, nor Hugh either. We took that wine-ship to go to Bordeaux; but the wind failed while we were yet in sight of Pevensey, a thick mist hid us, and we drifted with the tide along the cliffs to the west. Our company was, for the most part, merchants returning to France, and we were laden with wool and there were three couple of tall hunting-dogs chained to the rail. Their master was a knight of Artois. His name I never learned, but his shield bore gold pieces on a red ground, and he limped, much as I do, from a wound which he had got in his youth at Mantes siege. He served the Duke of Burgundy against the Moors in Spain, and was returning to that war with his dogs. He sang us strange Moorish songs that first night, and half persuaded us to go with him. I was on pilgrimage to forget – which is what no pilgrimage brings. I think I would have gone, but . . .

"Look you how the life and fortune of man changes! Towards morning a Dane ship, rowing silently, struck against us in the mist, and while we rolled hither and yon Hugh, leaning over the rail, fell outboard. I leaped after him, and we two tumbled aboard the Dane, and were caught and bound ere we could rise. Our own ship was swallowed up in the mist. I judge the Knight of the Gold Pieces muzzled his dogs with his cloak, lest they should give tongue and betray the merchants, for I heard their baying suddenly stop.

"We lay bound among the benches till morning, when the Danes dragged us to the high deck by the steering place, and their captain – Witta, he was called – turned us over with his foot. Bracelets of gold from elbow to armpit he wore, and his red hair was long as a woman''s, and came down in plaited locks on his shoulder. He was stout, with bowed legs and long arms. He spoiled us of all we had, but when he laid hand on Hugh's sword and saw the runes on the blade hastily he thrust it back. Yet his covetousness overcame him and he tried again and again, and the third time the Sword sang loud and angrily, so that the rowers leaned on their oars to listen. Here they all spoke together, screaming like gulls, and a Yellow Man, such as I have never seen, came to the high deck and cut our bonds. He was yellow – not from sickness, but by nature – yellow as honey, and his eyes stood endwise in his head."

"How do you mean?" said Una, her chin on her hand.

"Thus," said Sir Richard. He put a finger to the corner of each eye, and pushed it up till his eyes narrowed to slits.

"Why, you look just like a Chinaman!" cried Dan. "Was the man a Chinaman?"

"I know not what that may be. Witta had found him half dead among ice on the shores of Muscovy. We thought he was a devil. He crawled before us and brought food in a silver dish which these sea-wolves had robbed from some rich abbey, and Witta with his own hands gave us wine. He spoke a little in French, a little in South Saxon, and much in the Northman's tongue. We asked him to set us ashore, promising to pay him better ransom than he would get price if he sold us to the Moors – as once befell a knight of my acquaintance sailing from Flushing.

"'Not by my father Guthrum's head,' said he. 'The Gods sent ye into my ship for a luck offering.'

"At this I quaked, for I knew it was still the Danes' custom to sacrifice captives to their Gods for fair weather.

"'A plague on thy four long bones!' said Hugh. 'What profit canst thou make of poor old pilgrims that can neither work nor fight?'

"'Gods forbid I should fight against thee, poor Pilgrim with the Singing Sword,' said he. 'Come with us and be poor no more. Thy teeth are far apart, which is a sure sign thou wilt travel and grow rich.'

"'What if we will not come?' said Hugh.

"'Swim to England or France,' said Witta. 'We are midway between the two. Unless ye choose to drown yourselves no hair of your head will be harmed here aboard. We think ye bring us luck, and I myself know the runes on that Sword are good.' He turned and bade them hoist sail.

"Hereafter all made way for us as we walked about the ship, and the ship was full of wonders."

"What was she like?" said Dan.

"Long, low, and narrow, bearing one mast with a red sail, and rowed by fifteen oars a side," the knight answered. "At her bows was a deck under which men might lie, and at her stern another shut off by a painted door from the rowers' benches. Here Hugh and I slept, with Witta and the Yellow

Man, upon tapestries as soft as wool. I remember" – he laughed to himself – "when first we entered there a loud voice cried, 'Out swords! Out swords! Kill, kill!' Seeing us start Witta laughed, and showed us it was but a great-beaked grey bird with a red tail. He sat her on his shoulder, and she called for bread and wine hoarsely, and prayed him to kiss her. Yet she was no more than a silly bird. But – ye knew this?" He looked at their smiling faces.

"We weren't laughing at you," said Una. "That must have been a parrot. It's just what Pollies do."

"So we learned later. But here is another marvel. The Yellow Man, whose name was Kitai, had with him a brown box. In the box was a blue bowl with red marks upon the rim, and within the bowl, hanging from a fine thread, was a piece of iron no thicker than that grass stem, and as long, maybe, as my spur, but straight. In this iron, said Witta, abode an Evil Spirit which Kitai, the Yellow Man, had brought by Art Magic out of his own country that lay three years' journey southward. The Evil Spirit strove day and night to return to his country, and therefore, look you, the iron needle pointed continually to the South."

"South?" said Dan suddenly, and put his hand into his pocket.

"With my own eyes I saw it. Every day and all day long, though the ship rolled, though the sun and the moon and the stars were hid, this blind Spirit in the iron knew whither it would go, and strained to the South. Witta called it the Wise Iron, because it showed him his way across the unknowable seas." Again Sir Richard looked keenly at the children. "How think ye? Was it sorcery?"

"Was it anything like this?" Dan fished out his old brass pocket-compass, that generally lived with his knife and key-ring. "The glass has got cracked, but the needle waggles all right, sir."

The knight drew a long breath of wonder. "Yes, yes! The

Wise Iron shook and swung in just this fashion. Now it is still. Now it points to the South."

"North," said Dan.

"Nay, South! There is the South," said Sir Richard. Then they both laughed, for naturally when one end of a straight compass-needle points to the North, the other must point to the South.

"Té," said Sir Richard, clicking his tongue. "There can be no sorcery if a child carries it. Wherefore does it point South – or North?"

"Father says that nobody knows," said Una.

Sir Richard looked relieved. "Then it may still be magic. It was magic to *us*. And so we voyaged. When the wind served we hoisted sail, and lay all up along the windward rail, our shields on our backs to break the spray. When it failed, they rowed with long oars; the Yellow Man sat by the Wise Iron, and Witta steered. At first I feared the great white-flowering waves, but as I saw how wisely Witta led his ship among them I grew bolder. Hugh liked it well from the first. My skill is not upon the water; and rocks and whirlpools such as we saw by the West Isles of France, where an oar caught on a rock and broke, are much against my stomach. We sailed South across a stormy sea, where by moonlight, between clouds, we saw a Flanders ship roll clean over and sink. Again, though Hugh laboured with Witta all night, I lay under the deck with the Talking Bird, and cared not whether I lived or died. There is a sickness of the sea which for three days is pure death! When we next saw land Witta said it was Spain, and we stood out to sea. That coast was full of ships busy in the Duke's war against the Moors, and we feared to be hanged by the Duke's men or sold into slavery by the Moors. So we put into a small harbour which Witta knew. At night men came down with loaded mules, and Witta exchanged amber out of the North against little wedges of iron and packets of beads in earthen pots. The pots he put under the decks, and the wedges of iron he laid on the bottom of the ship after he had cast out the stones and shingle which till then had been our ballast. Wine, too, he bought for lumps of sweet-smelling grey amber – a little morsel no bigger than a thumb-nail purchased a cask of wine. But I speak like a merchant."

"No, no! Tell us what you had to eat," cried Dan.

"Meat dried in the sun, and dried fish and ground beans, Witta took in; and corded frails of a certain sweet, soft fruit, which the Moors use, which is like paste of figs, but with thin, long stones. Aha! Dates is the name.

"'Now,' said Witta, when the ship was loaded, 'I counsel you strangers to pray to your Gods, for, from here on, our road is No Man's road.' He and his men killed a black goat for sacrifice on the bows; and the Yellow Man brought out a small, smiling image of dull-green stone and burned incense before it. Hugh and I commended ourselves to God, and Saint Barnabas, and Our Lady of the Assumption, who was specially dear to my Lady. We were not young, but I think no shame to say when as we drove out of that secret harbour at sunrise over a still sea, we two rejoiced and sang as did the knights of old when they followed our great Duke to England. Yet was our leader an heathen pirate; all our proud fleet but one galley perilously overloaded; for guidance we leaned on a pagan sorcerer; and our port was beyond the world's end. Witta told us that his father Guthrum had once in his life rowed along the shores of Africa to a land where naked men sold gold for iron and beads. There had he bought much gold, and no few elephants' teeth, and thither by help of the Wise Iron would Witta go. Witta feared nothing – except to be poor.

"'My father told me,' said Witta, 'that a great Shoal runs three days' sail out from that land, and south of the shoal lies a Forest which grows in the sea. South and east of the Forest my father came to a place where the men hid gold in their hair; but all that country, he said, was full of Devils who lived in trees, and tore folk limb from limb. How think ye?'

"'Gold or no gold,' said Hugh, fingering his sword, 'it is a joyous venture. Have at these Devils of thine, Witta!'

"'Venture!' said Witta sourly. 'I am only a poor sea-thief. I do not set my life adrift on a plank for joy, or the venture. Once I beach ship again at Stavanger, and feel the wife's arms round my neck, I'll seek no more ventures. A ship is heavier care than a wife or cattle.'

"He leaped down among the rowers, chiding them for their little strength and their great stomachs. Yet Witta was a wolf in fight, and a very fox in cunning.

"We were driven South by a storm, and for three days and three nights he took the stern-oar, and threddled the long-ship through the sea. When it rose beyond measure he brake a pot of whale's oil upon the water, which wonder-fully smoothed it, and in that anointed patch he turned her head to the wind and threw out oars at the end of a rope, to make, he said, an anchor at which we lay rolling sorely, but dry. This craft his father Guthrum had shown him. He knew, too, all the Leech-Book of Bald, who was a wise doctor, and he knew the Ship-Book of Hlaf the Woman, who robbed Egypt. He knew all the care of a ship.

"After the storm we saw a mountain whose top was cov-ered with snow and pierced the clouds. The grasses under this mountain, boiled and eaten, are a good cure for sore-ness of the gums and swelled ankles. We lay there eight days, till men in skins threw stones at us. When the heat in-creased Witta spread a cloth on bent sticks above the row-ers, for the wind failed between the Island of the Mountain and the shore of Africa, which is east of it. That shore is sandy, and we rowed along it within three bowshots. Here we saw whales, and fish in the shape of shields, but longer than our ship. Some slept, some opened their mouths at us, and some danced on the hot waters. The water was hot to the hand, and the sky was hidden by hot, grey mists, out of which blew a fine dust that whitened our hair and beards of a morning. Here, too, were fish that flew in the air like birds. They would fall on the laps of the rowers, and when we went ashore we would roast and eat them."

The knight paused to see if the children doubted him, but they only nodded and said, "Go on."

"The yellow land lay on our left, the grey sea on our right. Knight though I was, I pulled my oar amongst the rowers. I caught seaweed and dried it, and stuffed it between the pots of beads lest they should break. Knighthood is for the land. At sea, look you, a man is but a spurless rider on a bridleless horse. I learned to make strong knots in ropes – yes, and to join two ropes end to end, so that even Witta could scarcely see where they had been married. But Hugh had tenfold more sea-cunning than I. Witta gave him charge of the rowers of the left side. Thorkild of Borkum, a man with a broken nose, that wore a Norman steel cap, had the rowers of the right, and each side rowed and sang against the other. They saw that no man was idle. Truly, as Hugh said, and Witta would laugh at him, a ship is all more care than a Manor.

"How? Thus. There was water to fetch from the shore when we could find it, as well as wild fruit and grasses, and sand for scrubbing of the decks and benches to keep them sweet. Also we hauled the ship out on low islands and emptied all her gear, even to the iron wedges, and burned off the weed, that had grown on her, with torches of rush, and smoked below the decks with rushes dampened in salt water, as Hlaf the Woman orders in her Ship-Book. Once when we were thus stripped, and the ship lay propped on her keel, the bird cried, 'Out swords!' as though she saw an enemy. Witta vowed he would wring her neck."

"Poor Polly! Did he?" said Una.

"Nay. She was the ship's-bird. She could call all the rowers by name . . . Those were good days – for a wifeless man – with Witta and his heathen – beyond the world's end . . . After many weeks we came on the great Shoal which stretched, as Witta's father had said, far out to sea. We skirted it till we were giddy with the sight and dizzy with the sound of bars and breakers, and when we reached land again we found a naked black people dwelling among woods, who for one wedge of iron loaded us with fruits and grasses and eggs. Witta scratched his head at them in sign he would buy gold. They had no gold, but they understood the sign (all the gold traders hide their gold in their thick hair), for they pointed along the coast. They beat, too, on their chests with their clenched hands, and that, if we had known it, was an evil sign."

"What did it mean?" said Dan.

"Patience. Ye shall hear. We followed the coast eastward sixteen days (counting time by sword-cuts on the helm-rail) till we came to the Forest in the Sea. Trees grew there out of mud, arched upon lean and high roots, and many muddy waterways ran all whither into darkness, under the trees. Here we lost the sun. We followed the winding channels between the trees, and where we could not row we laid hold of the crusted roots and hauled ourselves along. The water was foul, and great glittering flies tormented us. Morning and evening a blue mist covered the mud, which bred fevers. Four of our rowers sickened, and were bound to their benches, lest they should leap overboard and be eaten by the monsters of the mud. The Yellow Man lay sick beside the Wise Iron, rolling his head and talking in his own tongue. Only the Bird throve. She sat on Witta's shoulder and screamed in that noisome, silent darkness. Yes; I think it was the silence we most feared."

He paused to listen to the comfortable home noises of the brook.

"When we had lost count of time among those black gullies and swashes we heard, as it were, a drum beat far off, and following it we broke into a broad, brown river by a hut in a clearing among fields of pumpkins. We thanked God to see the sun again. The people of the village gave the good welcome, and Witta scratched his head at them (for gold), and showed them our iron and beads. They ran to the bank – we were still in the ship – and pointed to our swords and bows, for always when near shore we lay armed. Soon they fetched store of gold in bars and in dust from their huts, and some great blackened elephants' teeth. These they piled on the bank, as though to tempt us, and made signs of dealing blows in battle, and pointed up to the tree-tops, and to the forest behind. Their captain or chief sorcerer then beat on his chest with his fists, and gnashed his teeth.

"Said Thorkild of Borkum: 'Do they mean we must fight for all this gear?' and he half drew sword.

"'Nay,' said Hugh. 'I think they ask us to league against some enemy.'

"'I like this not,' said Witta, of a sudden. 'Back into midstream.'

"So we did, and sat still all, watching the black folk and the gold they piled on the bank. Again we heard drums beat in the forest, and the people fled to their huts, leaving the gold unguarded.

"Then Hugh, at the bows, pointed without speech, and we saw a great Devil come out of the forest. He shaded his brows with his hand, and moistened his pink tongue between his lips – thus."

"A Devil!" said Dan, delightfully horrified.

"Yea. Taller than a man; covered with reddish hair. When he had well regarded our ship, he beat on his chest with his fists till it sounded like rolling drums, and came to the bank swinging all his body between his long arms, and gnashed his teeth at us. Hugh loosed arrow, and pierced him through the throat. He fell roaring, and three other Devils ran out of the forest and hauled him into a tall tree out of sight. Anon they cast down the blood-stained arrow, and lamented together among the leaves.

"Witta saw the gold on the bank; he was loath to leave it. 'Sirs,' said he (no man had spoken till then), 'yonder is what we have come so far and so painfully to find, laid out to our very hand. Let us row in while these Devils bewail themselves, and at least bear off what we may.'

"Bold as a wolf, cunning as a fox was Witta! He set four archers on the fore-deck to shoot the Devils if they should leap from the tree, which was close to the bank. He manned ten oars a side, and bade them watch his hand to row in or back out, and so coaxed he them toward the bank. But none would set foot ashore, though the gold was within ten paces. No man is hasty to his hanging! They whimpered at their oars like beaten hounds, and Witta bit his fingers for rage."

"Said Hugh of a sudden, 'Hark!' At first we thought it was the buzzing of the glittering flies on the water; but it grew loud and fierce, so that all men heard."

"What?" said Dan and Una.

"It was the Sword." Sir Richard patted the smooth hilt. "It sang as a Dane sings before battle. 'I go,' said Hugh, and he leaped from the bows and fell among the gold. I was afraid to my four bones' marrow, but for shame's sake I followed, and Thorkild of Borkum leaped after me. None other came. 'Blame me not,' cried Witta behind us, 'I must abide by my ship.' We three had no time to blame or praise. We stooped to the gold and threw it back over our shoulders, one hand on our swords and one eye on the tree, which nigh overhung us.

"I know not how the devils leaped down, or how the fight began. I heard Hugh cry: 'Out! out!' as though he were at Santlache again; I saw Thorkild's steel cap smitten off his head by a great hairy hand, and I felt an arrow from the ship whistle past my ear. They say that till Witta took his sword to the rowers he could not bring his ship inshore; and each one of the four archers said afterwards that he alone had pierced the Devil that fought me. I do not know. I went to it in my mail-shirt, which saved my skin. With long-sword and belt-dagger I fought for the life against a Devil whose very feet were hands, and who whirled me back and forth like a dead branch. He had me by the waist, my arms to my side, when an arrow from the ship pierced him between the shoulders, and he loosened grip. I passed my sword twice through him, and he crutched himself away between his long arms, coughing and moaning. Next, as I remember, I saw Thorkild of Borkum, bare-headed and smiling, leaping up and down before a Devil that leaped and gnashed his teeth. Then Hugh passed, his sword shifted to his left hand, and I wondered why I had not known that Hugh was a left-handed man; and thereafter I remembered nothing till I felt spray on my face, and we were in sunshine on the open sea. That was twenty days after."

"What had happened? Did Hugh die?" the children asked.

"Never was such a fight fought by christened man," said Sir Richard. "An arrow from the ship had saved me from my Devil, and Thorkild of Borkum had given back before his Devil, till the bowmen on the ship could shoot it all full of arrows from near by; but Hugh's Devil was cunning, and had kept behind trees, where no arrow could reach. Body to body there, by stark strength of sword and hand, had Hugh slain him, and, dying, the Thing had clenched his teeth on the sword. Judge what teeth they were!"

Sir Richard turned the sword again that the children might see the two great chiselled gouges on either side of the blade.

"Those same teeth met in Hugh's right arm and side," Sir

Richard went on. "I? Oh, I had no more than a broken foot and a fever. Thorkild's ear was bitten, but Hugh's arm and side clean withered away. I saw him where he lay along, sucking a fruit in his left hand. His flesh was wasted off his bones, his hair was patched with white, and his hand was blue-veined like a woman's. He put his left arm round my neck and whispered, 'Take my sword. It has been thine since Hastings, O my brother, but I can never hold hilt again.' We lay there on the high deck talking of Santlache, and, I think, of every day since Santlache, and it came so that we both wept. I was weak, and he little more than a shadow.

"'Nay – nay,' said Witta, at the helm rail. 'Gold is a good right arm to any man. Look – look at the gold!' He bade Thorkild show us the gold and the elephants' teeth, as though we had been children. He had brought away all the gold on the bank, and twice as much more, that the people of the village gave him for slaying the Devils. They worshipped us as Gods, Thorkild told me: it was one of their old women healed up Hugh's poor arm."

"How much gold did you get?" asked Dan.

"How can I say? Where we came out with wedges of iron under the rowers' feet we returned with wedges of gold hidden beneath planks. There was dust of gold in packages where we slept and along the side, and cross-wise under the benches we lashed the blackened elephants' teeth.

"'I had sooner have my right arm,' said Hugh, when he had seen all.

"'Ahai! That was my fault,' said Witta. 'I should have taken ransom and landed you in France when first you came aboard, ten months ago.'

"'It is over-late now,' said Hugh, laughing.

"Witta plucked at his long shoulder lock. 'But think!' said he. 'If I had let ye go – which I swear I would never have done, for I love ye more than brothers – if I had let ye go, by now ye might have been horribly slain by some mere Moor in the Duke of Burgundy's war, or ye might have been murdered by land-thieves, or ye might have died of the plague at an inn. Think of this and do not blame me overmuch, Hugh. See! I will only take a half of the gold.'

"'I blame thee not at all, Witta,' said Hugh. 'It was a joyous venture, and we thirty-five here have done what never men have done. If I live till England, I will build me a stout keep over Dallington out of my share.'

"'I will buy cattle and amber and warm red cloth for the wife,' said Witta, 'and I will hold all the land at the head of Stavanger Fiord. Many will fight for me now. But first we must turn North, and with this honest treasure aboard I pray we meet no pirate ships.'

"We did not laugh. We were careful. We were afraid lest we should lose one grain of our gold, for which we had fought Devils.

"Where is the Sorcerer?" said I, for Witta was looking at the Wise Iron in the box, and I could not see the Yellow Man.

"He has gone to his own country," said he. "He rose up in the night while we were beating out of that forest in the mud, and said that he could see it behind the trees. He leaped out on the mud, and did not answer when we called; so we called no more. He left the Wise Iron, which is all that I care for – and see, the Spirit still points to the South."

"We were troubled for fear that the Wise Iron should fail us now that its Yellow Man had gone, and when we saw the Spirit still served us we grew afraid of too strong winds, and of shoals, and of careless leaping fish, and of all the people on all the shores where we landed."

"Why?" said Dan.

"Because of the gold – because of our gold. Gold changes men altogether. Thorkild of Borkum did not change. He laughed at Witta for his fears, and at us for our counselling Witta to furl sail when the ship pitched at all.

"'Better be drowned out of hand,' said Thorkild of Borkum, 'than go tied to a deck-load of yellow dust.'

"He was a landless man, and had been slave to some King in the East. He would have beaten out the gold into deep bands to put round the oars, and round the prow."

"Yet, though he vexed himself for the gold, Witta waited upon Hugh like a woman, lending him his shoulder when the ship rolled, and tying of ropes from side to side that Hugh might hold by them. But for Hugh, he said – and so did all his men – they would never have won the gold. I remember Witta made a little, thin gold ring for our Bird to swing in.

"Three months we rowed and sailed and went ashore for fruits or to clean the ship. When we saw wild horse-men, riding among sand-dunes, flourishing spears, we knew we were on the Moors' coast, and stood over north to Spain; and a strong south-west wind bore us in ten days to a coast of high red rocks, where we heard a hunting-horn blow among the yellow gorse and knew it was England.

"'Now find ye Pevensey yourselves,' said Witta. 'I love not these narrow ship-filled seas.'

"He set the dried, salted head of the Devil, which Hugh had killed, high on our prow, and all boats fled from us. Yet, for our gold's sake, we were more afraid than they. We crept along the coast by night till we came to the chalk cliffs, and so east to Pevensey. Witta would not come ashore with us, though Hugh promised him wine at Dallington enough to swim in. He was on fire to see his wife, and ran into the Marsh after sunset, and there he left us and our share of gold, and backed out on the same tide. He made no promise; he swore no oath; he looked for no thanks; but to Hugh, an armless man, and to me, an old cripple whom he could have flung into the sea, he passed over wedge upon wedge, packet upon packet of gold and dust of gold, and only ceased when we would take no more.

As he stooped from the rail to bid us farewell he stripped off his right-arm bracelets and put them all on Hugh's left, and he kissed Hugh on the cheek. I think when Thorkild of Borkum bade the rowers give way we were near weeping. It is true that Witta was an heathen and a pirate; true it is he held us by force many months in his ship, but I loved that bow-legged, blue-eyed man for his great boldness, his cunning, his skill, and, beyond all, for his simplicity."

"Did he get home all right?" said Dan.

"I never knew. We saw him hoist sail under the moon-track and stand away. I have prayed that he found his wife and the children."

"And what did you do?"

"We waited on the Marsh till the day. Then I sat by the gold, all tied in an old sail, while Hugh went to Pevensey, and De Aquila sent us horses."

Sir Richard crossed hands on his sword-hilt, and stared down stream through the soft warm shadows.

"A whole shipload of gold!" said Una, looking at the little *Golden Hind.* "But I'm glad I didn't see the Devils."

"I don't believe they were Devils," Dan whispered back.

"Eh?" said Sir Richard. "Witta's father warned him they were unquestionable Devils. One must believe one's father, and not one's children. What were my Devils, then?"

Dan flushed all over. "I – I only thought," he stammered; "I've got a book called *The Gorilla Hunters* – it's a continuation of *Coral Island,* sir – and it says there that the gorillas (they're big monkeys, you know) were always chewing iron up."

"Not always," said Una. "Only twice." They had been reading *The Gorilla Hunters* in the orchard.

"Well, anyhow, they always drummed on their chests, like Sir Richard's did, before they went for people. And they built houses in trees, too."

"Ha!" Sir Richard opened his eyes. "Houses like flat

nests did our Devils make, where their imps lay and looked at us. I did not see them (I was sick after the fight), but Witta told me, and, lo, ye know it also? Wonderful! Were our Devils only nest-building apes? Is there no sorcery left in the world?"

"I don't know," answered Dan, uncomfortably. "I've seen a man take rabbits out of a hat, and he told us we could see how he did it, if we watched hard. And we did."

"But we didn't," said Una, sighing. "Oh! there's Puck!"

The little fellow, brown and smiling, peered between two stems of an ash, nodded, and slid down the bank into the cool beside them.

"No sorcery, Sir Richard?" he laughed, and blew on a full dandelion head he had picked.

"They tell me that Witta's Wise Iron was a toy. The boy carries such an iron with him. They tell me our Devils were apes, called gorillas!" said Sir Richard, indignantly.

"That is the sorcery of books," said Puck. "I warned thee they were wise children. All people can be wise by reading of books."

"But are the books true?" Sir Richard frowned. "I like not all this reading and writing."

"Ye-es," said Puck, holding the naked dandelion head at arm's length. "But if we hang all fellows who write falsely, why did De Aquila not begin with Gilbert the Clerk? *He* was false enough."

"Poor false Gilbert. Yet, in his fashion, he was bold," said Sir Richard.

"What did he do?" said Dan.

"He wrote," said Sir Richard. "Is the tale meet for children, think you?" He looked at Puck; but "Tell us! Tell us!" cried Dan and Una together.

THORKILD'S SONG

There's no wind along these seas,
 Out oars for Stavanger!
 Forward all for Stavanger!
So we must wake the white-ash breeze,
 Let fall for Stavanger!
 A long pull for Stavanger!
Oh, hear the benches creak and strain!
 (A long pull for Stavanger!)
She thinks she smells the Northland rain!
 (A long pull for Stavanger!)

She thinks she smells the Northland snow,
And she's as glad as we to go.

She thinks she smells the Northland rime,
And the dear dark nights of winter-time.

Her very bolts are sick for shore,
And we – we want it ten times more!

So all you Gods that love brave men,
Send us a three-reef gale again!

Send us a gale, and watch us come,
With close-cropped canvas slashing home!

But – there's no wind in all these seas.
 A long pull for Stavanger!
So we must wake the white-ash breeze,
 A long pull for Stavanger!

Old Men at Pevensey

"It has naught to do with apes or Devils," Sir Richard went on, in an undertone. "It concerns De Aquila, than whom there was never bolder nor craftier, nor more hardy knight born. And remember he was an old, old man at that time."

"When?" said Dan.

"When we came back from sailing with Witta."

"What did you do with your gold?" said Dan.

"Have patience. Link by link is chain-mail made. I will tell all in its place. We bore the gold to Pevensey on horse-back – three loads of it – and then up to the north chamber, above the Great Hall of Pevensey Castle, where De Aquila lay in winter. He sat on his bed like a little white falcon, turning his head swiftly from the one to the other as we told our tale. Jehan the Crab, an old sour man-at-arms, guarded the stairway, but De Aquila bade him wait at the stair-foot, and let down both leather curtains over the door. It was Jehan whom De Aquila had sent to us with the horses, and only Jehan had loaded the gold. When our story was told, De Aquila gave us the news of England, for we were as men waked from a year-long sleep. The Red King was dead – slain (ye remember?) the day we set sail – and Henry, his younger brother, had made himself King of England over the head of Robert of Normandy. This was the very thing that the Red King had done to Robert when our Great William died. Then Robert of Normandy, mad, as De Aquila said, at twice missing of this kingdom, had sent an army against England, which army had been well beaten back to their ships at Portsmouth. A littler earlier, and Witta's ship would have rowed through them.

"'And now,' said De Aquila, 'half the great Barons of the North and West are out against the King between Salisbury and Shrewsbury, and half the other half wait to see which way the game shall go. They say Henry is overly English for their stomachs, because he hath married an English wife and she hath coaxed him to give back their old laws to our Saxons. (Better ride a horse on the bit he knows, *I* say!) But that is only a cloak to their falsehood.' He cracked his finger on the table, where the wine was spilt, and thus he spoke:

"'William crammed us Norman barons full of good English acres after Santlache. I had my share too,' he said, and clapped Hugh on the shoulder; 'but I warned him – I warned him before Odo rebelled – that he should have bidden the Barons give up their lands and lordships in Normandy if they would be English lords. Now they are all but princes both in England and Normandy – trencher-fed hounds, with a foot in one trough and both eyes on the other! Robert of Normandy has sent them word that if they do not fight for him in England he will sack and harry out their lands in Normandy. Therefore Clare has risen, FitzOsborne has risen, Montgomery has risen – whom our First William made an English Earl. Even D'Arcy is out with his men, whose father I remember a little hedge-sparrow knight near by Caen. If Henry wins, the Barons can still flee to Normandy, where Robert will welcome them. If Henry loses, Robert, he says, will give them more lands in England. Oh, a pest – a pest on Normandy, for she will be our England's curse this many a long year!'

"'Amen,' said Hugh. 'But will the war come our ways, think you?'

"'Not from the North,' said De Aquila. 'But the sea is always open. If the Barons gain the upper hand Robert will send another army into England for sure, and this time I think he will land here – where his father, the Conqueror,

landed. Ye have brought your pigs to a pretty market! Half
England alight, and gold enough on the ground" – he
stamped on the bars beneath the table – 'to set every sword
in Christendom fighting.'

"'What is to do?' said Hugh. 'I have no keep at
Dallington; and if we buried it, whom could we trust?'

"'Me,' said De Aquila. 'Pevensey walls are strong. No
man but Jehan, who is my dog, knows what is between
them.' He drew a curtain by the shot-window and showed
us the shaft of a well in the thickness of the wall.

"'I made it for a drinking-well,' he said, 'but we found
salt water, and it rises and falls with the tide. Hark!' We
heard the water whistle and blow at the bottom. 'Will it
serve?' said he.

"'Needs must,' said Hugh. 'Our lives are in thy hands.'
So we lowered all the gold down except one small chest of
it by De Aquila's bed, which we kept as much for his delight in its weight and colour as for any of our needs.

"'In the morning, ere we rode to our Manors,' he said: 'I
do not say farewell; because ye will return and bide here.
Not for love nor for sorrow, but to be with the gold. Have a
care,' he said, laughing, 'lest I use it to make myself Pope.
Trust me not, but return'"

Sir Richard paused and smiled sadly.

"In seven days, then, we returned from our Manors –
from the Manors which had been ours."

"And were the children quite well?" said Una.

"My sons were young. Land and governance belong by
right to young men." Sir Richard was talking to himself "It
would have broken their hearts if we had taken back our
Manors. They made us great welcome, but we could see –
Hugh and I could see – that our day was done. I was a crip-
ple and he a one-armed man. No!" He shook his head.
"And therefore" – he raised his voice – "we rode back to
Pevensey."

"I'm sorry," said Una, for the knight seemed very sorrowful.

"Little maid, it all passed long ago. They were young; we were old. We let them rule the Manors. 'Aha!' cried De Aquila from his shot-window, when we dismounted. 'Back again to earth, old foxes?' but when we were in his chamber above the Hall he puts his arms about us and says, 'Welcome, ghosts! Welcome, poor ghosts!' . . . Thus it fell out that we were rich beyond belief, and lonely. And lonely!"

"What did you do?" said Dan.

"We watched for Robert of Normandy," said the knight. "De Aquila was like Witta. He suffered no idleness. In fair weather we would ride along between Bexlei on the one side, to Cuckmere on the other – sometimes with hawk, sometimes with hound (there are stout hares both on the Marsh and the Downland), but always with an eye to the sea, for fear of fleets from Normandy. In foul weather he would walk on the top of his tower, frowning against the rain – peering here and pointing there. It always vexed him to think how Witta's ship had come and gone without his knowledge. When the wind ceased and ships anchored, to the wharf's edge he would go and, leaning on his sword among the stinking fish, would call to the mariners for their news from France. His other eye he kept landward for word of Henry's war against the Barons.

"Many brought him news – jongleurs, harpers, pedlars, sutlers, priests and the like; and, though he was secret enough in small things, yet, if their news misliked him, then, regarding neither time nor place nor people, he would curse our King Henry for a fool or a babe. I have heard him cry aloud by the fishing boats: 'If I were King of England I would do thus and thus'; and when I rode out to see that the warning-beacons were laid and dry, he hath often called to me from the shot-window: 'Look to it, Richard! Do not copy our blind King, but see with thine own eyes and feel

with thine own hands.' I do not think he knew any sort of
fear. And so we lived at Pevensey, in the little chamber
above the Hall.

"One foul night came word that a messenger of the King
waited below. We were chilled after a long riding in the fog
towards Bexlei, which is an easy place for ships to land. De
Aquila sent word the man might either eat with us or wait
till we had fed. Anon Jehan, at the stairhead, cried that he
had called for horse, and was gone. 'Pest on him!' said De
Aquila. 'I have more to do than to shiver in the Great Hall
for every gadling the King sends. Left he no word?'

"'None,' said Jehan, 'except' – he had been with De
Aquila at Santlache – 'except he said that if an old dog
could not learn new tricks it was time to sweep out the
kennel.'

"'Oho!' said De Aquila, rubbing his nose, 'to whom did
he say that?'

"'To his beard, chiefly, but some to his horse's flank as he
was girthing up. I followed him out,' said Jehan the Crab.

"'What was his shield mark?'

"'Gold horseshoes on black,' said the Crab.

"'That is one of Fulke's men,' said De Aquila.

Puck broke in very gently, "Gold horseshoes on black is
not the Fulkes' shield. The Fulkes' arms are – "

The knight waved one hand statelily.

"Thou knowest that evil man's true name," he replied,
"but I have chosen to call him Fulke because I promised
him I would not tell the story of his wickedness so that any
man might guess it. I have changed *all* the names in my
tale. His children's children may be still alive."

"True – true," said Puck, smiling softly. "It is knightly to
keep faith – even after a thousand years."

Sir Richard bowed a little and went on:

"'Gold horseshoes on black?' said De Aquila. 'I had
heard Fulke had joined the Barons, but if this is true our

King must be of the upper hand. No matter, all Fulkes are faithless. Still, I would not have sent the man away empty.'

"'He fed,' said Jehan. 'Gilbert the Clerk fetched him meat and wine from the kitchens. He ate at Gilbert's table.'

"This Gilbert was a clerk from Battle Abbey, who kept the accounts of the Manor of Pevensey. He was tall and pale-coloured, and carried those new-fashioned beads for counting of prayers. They were large brown nuts or seeds, and hanging from his girdle with his pen and ink-horn they clashed when he walked. His place was in the great fire-place. There was his table of accounts, and there he lay o' nights. He feared the hounds in the Hall that came nosing after bones or to sleep on the warm ashes, and would slash at them with his beads – like a woman. When De Aquila sat in Hall to do justice, take fines, or grant lands, Gilbert would so write it in the Manor-roll. But it was none of his work to feed our guests, or to let them depart without his lord's knowledge.

"Said De Aquila, after Jehan was gone down the stair: 'Hugh, hast thou ever told my Gilbert thou canst read Latin hand-of-write?'

"'No,' said Hugh. 'He is no friend to me, or to Odo my hound either.' 'No matter,' said De Aquila. 'Let him never know thou canst tell one letter from its fellow, and' – there he yerked us in the ribs with his scabbard 'watch him, both of ye. There be devils in Africa, as I have heard, but by the Saints, there be greater devils in Pevensey!' And that was all he would say.

"It chanced, some small while afterwards, a Norman man-at-arms would wed a Saxon wench of the Manor, and Gilbert (we had watched him well since De Aquila spoke) doubted whether her folk were free or slave. Since De Aquila would give them a field of good land, if she were free, the matter came up at the justice in Great Hall before De Aquila. First the wench's father spoke; then her mother;

then all together, till the Hall rang and the hounds bayed.
De Aquila held up his hands. 'Write her free,' he called to
Gilbert by the fireplace. 'A' God's name write her free, before she deafens me! Yes, yes,' he said to the wench that
was on her knees at him; 'thou art Cerdic's sister, and own
cousin to the Lady of Mercia, if thou wilt be silent. In fifty
years there will be neither Norman nor Saxon, but all English,' said he, 'and *these* are the men that do our work!' He
clapped the man-at-arms that was Jehan's nephew on the
shoulder, and kissed the wench, and fretted with his feet
among the rushes to show it was finished. (The Great Hall
is always bitter cold.) I stood at his side; Hugh was behind
Gilbert in the fireplace making to play with wise rough
Odo. He signed to De Aquila, who bade Gilbert measure
the new field for the new couple. Out then runs our Gilbert
between man and maid, his beads clashing at his waist, and
the Hall being empty, we three sit by the fire.

"Said Hugh, leaning down to the hearthstones, 'I saw this
stone move under Gilbert's foot when Odo snuffed at it.
Look!' De Aquila digged in the ashes with his sword; the
stone tilted; beneath it lay a parchment folden, and the writing atop was: 'Words spoken against the King by our Lord
of Pevensey – the second part.'

"Here was set out (Hugh read it us whispering) every jest
De Aquila had made to us touching the King; every time he
had called out to me from the shot-window, and every time
he had said what he would do if he were King of England.
Yes, day by day had his daily speech, which he never
stinted, been set down by Gilbert, tricked out and twisted
from its true meaning, yet withal so cunningly that none
could deny who knew him that De Aquila had in some sort
spoken those words. Ye see?"

Dan and Una nodded.

"Yes," said Una gravely. "It isn't what you say so much.
It's what you mean when you say it. Like calling Dan a

beast in fun. Only grown-ups don't always understand."

"'He hath done this day by day before our very face?' said De Aquila.

"'Nay, hour by hour,' said Hugh. 'When De Aquila spoke even now, in the Hall, of Saxons and Normans, I saw Gilbert write on a parchment, which he kept beside the Manor roll, that De Aquila said soon there would be no Normans left in England if his men-at-arms did their work aright.'

"'Bones of the Saints!' said De Aquila. 'What avail is honour or a sword against a pen? Where did Gilbert hide that writing? He shall eat it.'

"'In his breast when he ran out,' said Hugh. 'Which made me look to see where he kept his finished stuff. When Odo scratched at this stone here, I saw his face change. So I was sure.'

"'He is bold,' said De Aquila. 'Do him justice. In his own fashion, my Gilbert is bold.'

"'Overbold,' said Hugh. 'Hearken here,' and he read: 'Upon the Feast of St Agatha, our Lord of Pevensey, lying in his upper chamber, being clothed in his second fur gown reversed with rabbit – '

"'Pest on him! He is not my tire-woman!' said De Aquila, and Hugh and I laughed.

"'Reversed with rabbit, seeing a fog over the marshes, did wake Sir Richard Dalyngridge, his drunken cup-mate' (here they laughed at me) and said, 'Peer out, old fox, for God is on the Duke of Normandy's side.'

"'So did I. It was a black fog. Robert could have landed ten thousand men, and we none the wiser. Does he tell how we were out all day riding the Marsh, and how I near perished in a quicksand, and coughed like a sick ewe for ten days after?' cried De Aquila.

"'No,' said Hugh. 'But here is the prayer of Gilbert himself to his master Fulke.'

"'Ah,' said De Aquila. 'Well I knew it was Fulke. What is the price of my blood?'

"'Gilbert prayeth that when our Lord of Pevensey is stripped of his lands on this evidence which Gilbert hath, with fear and pains, collected – '

"'Fear and pains is a true word,' said De Aquila, and sucked in his cheeks. 'But how excellent a weapon is a pen! I must learn it.'

"'He prays that Fulke will advance him from his present service to that honour in the Church which Fulke promised him. And lest Fulke should forget, he has written below, "To be Sacristan of Battle."'

"At this De Aquila whistled. 'A man who can plot against one lord can plot against another. When I am stripped of my lands Fulke will whip off my Gilbert's foolish head. None the less Battle needs a new Sacristan. They tell me the Abbot Henry keeps no sort of rule there.'

"'Let the Abbot wait,' said Hugh. 'It is our heads and our lands that are in danger. This parchment is the second part of the tale. The first has gone to Fulke, and so to the King, who will hold us traitors.'

"'Assuredly,' said De Aquila. 'Fulke's man took the first part that evening when Gilbert fed him, and our King is so beset by his brother and his Barons (small blame, too!) that he is mad with mistrust. Fulke has his ear, and pours poison into it. Presently the King gives him my land and yours. This is old,' and he leaned back and yawned.

"'And thou wilt surrender Pevensey without word or blow?' said Hugh. 'We Saxons will fight your King then. I will go warn my nephew at Dallington. Give me a horse!'

"'Give thee a toy and a rattle,' said De Aquila. 'Put back the parchment, and rake over the ashes. If Fulke is given my Pevensey, which is England's gate, what will he do with it? He is Norman at heart, and his heart is in Normandy, where he can kill peasants at his pleasure. He will open

England's gate to our sleepy Robert, as Odo and Mortain tried to do, and then there will be another landing and another Santlache. Therefore I cannot give up Pevensey.'

"'Good,' said we two.

"'Ah, but wait! If my King be made, on Gilbert's evidence, to mistrust me, he will send his men against me here, and while we fight, England's gate is left unguarded. Who will be the first to come through thereby? Even Robert of Normandy. Therefore I cannot fight my King.' He nursed his sword – thus.

"'This is saying and unsaying like a Norman,' said Hugh. 'What of our Manors?'

"'I do not think for myself,' said De Aquila, 'nor for our King, nor for your lands. I think for England, for whom neither King nor Baron thinks. I am not Norman, Sir Richard, nor Saxon, Sir Hugh. English am I.'

"'Saxon, Norman or English,' said Hugh, 'our lives are thine, however the game goes. When do we hang Gilbert?'

"'Never,' said De Aquila. 'Who knows, he may yet be Sacristan of Battle, for, to do him justice, he is a good writer. Dead men make dumb witnesses. Wait.'

"'But the King may give Pevensey to Fulke. And our Manors go with it,' said I. 'Shall we tell our sons?'

"'No. The King will not wake up a hornets' nest in the South till he has smoked out the bees in the North. He may hold me a traitor; but at least he sees I am not fighting against him; and every day that I lie still is so much gain to him while he fights the Barons. If he were wise he would wait till that war were over before he made new enemies. But I think Fulke will play upon him to send for me, and if I do not obey the summons, that will, to Henry's mind, be proof of my treason. But mere talk, such as Gilbert sends, is no proof nowadays. We Barons follow the Church, and, like Anselm, we speak what we please. Let us go about our day's dealings, and say naught to Gilbert.'

"'Then we do nothing?' said Hugh.

"'We wait,' said De Aquila. 'I am old, but still I find that the most grievous work I know.'

And so we found it, but in the end De Aquila was right.

"A little later in the year, armed men rode over the hill, the Golden Horseshoes flying behind the King's banner. Said De Aquila, at the window of our chamber: 'How did I tell you? Here comes Fulke himself to spy out his new lands which our King hath promised him if he can bring proof of my treason.'

"'How dost thou know?' said Hugh.

"'Because that is what I would do if I were Fulke, but I should have brought more men. My roan horse to your old shoes,' said he, 'Fulke brings me the King's Summons to leave Pevensey and join the war.' He sucked in his cheeks and drummed on the edge of the well-shaft, where the water sounded all hollow.

"'Shall we go?' said I.

"'Go! At this time of year? Stark madness,' said he. 'Take *me* from Pevensey to fisk and flyte through fern and forest, and in three days Robert's keels would be lying on Pevensey mud with ten thousand men! Who would stop them – Fulke?'

"The homs blew without, and anon Fulke cried the King's Summons at the great door, that De Aquila with all men and horse should join the King's camp at Salisbury.

"'How did I tell you?' said De Aquila. 'There are twenty Barons 'twixt here and Salisbury could give King Henry good land service, but he has been worked upon by Fulke to send South and call me – *me!* – off the Gate of England, when his enemies stand about to batter it in. See that Fulke's men lie in the big south barn,' said he. 'Give them drink, and when Fulke has eaten we will drink in my chamber. The Great Hall is too cold for old bones.'

"As soon as he was off-horse Fulke went to the chapel

with Gilbert to give thanks for his safe coming, and when he had eaten – he was a fat man, and rolled his eyes greedily at our good roast Sussex wheat-ears – we led him to the little upper chamber, whither Gilbert had already gone with the Manor-roll. I remember when Fulke heard the tide blow and whistle in the shaft he leaped back, and his long downturned stirrup-shoes caught in the rushes and he stumbled, so that Jehan behind him found it easy to knock his head against the wall."

"Did you know it was going to happen?" said Dan.

"Assuredly," said Sir Richard, with a sweet smile. "I put my foot on his sword and plucked away his dagger, but he knew not whether it was day or night for awhile. He lay rolling his eyes and bubbling with his mouth, and Jehan roped him like a calf. He was cased all in that new-fangled armour which we call lizard-mail. Not rings like my hauberk here" – Sir Richard tapped his chest – "but little pieces of dagger-proof steel overlapping on stout leather. We stripped it off (no need to spoil good harness by wetting it), and in the neck-piece De Aquila found the same folden piece of parchment which we had put back under the hearthstone.

"At this Gilbert would have run out. I laid my hand on his shoulder. It sufficed. He fell to trembling and praying on his beads.

"'Gilbert,' said De Aquila, 'here be more notable sayings and doings of our Lord of Pevensey for thee to write down. Take pen and ink-horn, Gilbert. We cannot all be Sacristans of Battle.'

"Said Fulke from the floor, 'Ye have bound a King's messenger. Pevensey shall burn for this.'

"'Maybe. I have seen it besieged once,' said De Aquila, 'but heart up, Fulke. I promise thee that thou shalt be hanged in the middle of the flames at the end of that siege, if I have to share my last loaf with thee; and that is more than Odo would have done when we starved out him and Mortain.'

"Then Fulke sat up and looked long and cunningly at De Aquila.

"'By the Saints,' said he, 'why didst thou not say thou wast on the Duke Robert's side at the first?'

"'Am I?' said De Aquila.

"Fulke laughed and said, 'No man who serves King Henry dare do this much to his messenger. When didst thou come over to the Duke? Let me up and we can smooth it out together.' And he smiled and becked and winked.

"'Yes, we will smooth it out,' said De Aquila. He nodded to me, and Jehan and I heaved up Fulke – he was a heavy man – and lowered him into the shaft by a rope, not so as to stand on our gold, but dangling by his shoulders a little above. It was turn of ebb, and the water came to his knees. He said nothing, but shivered somewhat.

"Then Jehan of a sudden beat down Gilbert's wrist with his sheathed dagger. 'Stop!' he said. 'He swallows his beads.'

"'Poison, belike,' said De Aquila. 'It is good for men who know too much. I have carried it these thirty years. Give me!'

"Then Gilbert wept and howled. De Aquila ran the beads through his fingers. The last one – I have said they were large nuts – opened in two halves on a pin, and there was a small folded parchment within. On it was written: *'The Old Dog goes to Salisbury to be beaten. I have his Kennel. Come quickly.'*

"'This is worse than poison,' said De Aquila very softly, and sucked in his cheeks. Then Gilbert grovelled in the rushes, and told us all he knew. The letter, as we guessed, was from Fulke to the Duke (and not the first that had passed between them); Fulke had given it to Gilbert in the chapel, and Gilbert thought to have taken it by morning to a certain fishing boat at the wharf, which trafficked between

Pevensey and the French shore. Gilbert was a false fellow, but he found time between his quakings and shakings to swear that the master of the boat knew nothing of the matter.

"'He hath called me shaved-head,' said Gilbert, 'and he hath thrown haddock-guts at me; but for all that, he is no traitor.'

"'I will have no clerk of mine mishandled or miscalled,' said De Aquila. 'That seaman shall be whipped at his own mast. Write me first a letter, and thou shalt bear it, with the order for the whipping, tomorrow to the boat.'

"At this Gilbert would have kissed De Aquila's hand he had not hoped to live until the morning – and when he trembled less he wrote a letter as from Fulke to the Duke, saying that the Kennel, which signified Pevensey, was shut, and that the Old Dog (which was De Aquila) sat outside it, and, moreover, that all had been betrayed.

"'Write to any man that all is betrayed,' said De Aquila, 'and even the Pope himself would sleep uneasily. Eh, Jehan? If one told thee all was betrayed, what wouldst thou do?'

"'I would run away,' said Jehan. 'It might be true.'

"'Well said,' quoth De Aquila. 'Write, Gilbert, that Montgomery, the great Earl, hath made his peace with the King, and that little D'Arcy, whom I hate, hath been hanged by the heels. We will give Robert full measure to chew upon. Write also that Fulke himself is sick to death of a dropsy.'

"'Nay!' cried Fulke, hanging in the well shaft. 'Drown me out of hand, but do not make a jest of me.'

"'Jest? I?' said De Aquila. 'I am but fighting for life and lands with a pen, as thou hast shown me, Fulke.'

"Then Fulke groaned, for he was cold, and, 'Let me confess,' said he.

"'Now, this is right neighbourly,' said De Aquila, leaning over the shaft. 'Thou hast read my sayings and doings – or at least the first part of them – and thou art minded to repay me with thy own doings and sayings. Take pen and ink-horn, Gilbert. Here is work that will not irk thee.'

"'Let my men go without hurt, and I will confess my treason against the King,' said Fulke.

"'Now, why has he grown so tender of his men of a sudden?' said Hugh to me; for Fulke had no name for mercy to his men. Plunder he gave them, but pity, none.

"'Té! Té!' said De Aquila. 'Thy treason was all confessed long ago by Gilbert. It would be enough to hang Montgomery himself.'

"'Nay; but spare my men,' said Fulke; and we heard him splash like a fish in a pond, for the tide was rising.

"'All in good time,' said De Aquila. 'The night is young; the wine is old; and we need only the merry tale. Begin the story of thy life since when thou wast a lad at Tours. Tell it nimbly!'

"'Ye shame me to my soul,' said Fulke.

"'Then I have done what neither King nor Duke could do,' said De Aquila. 'But begin, and forget nothing.'

"'Send thy man away,' said Fulke.

"'That much can I do,' said De Aquila. 'But, remember, I am like the Danes' King. I cannot turn the tide.'

"'How long will it rise?' said Fulke, and splashed anew.

"'For three hours,' said De Aquila. 'Time to tell all thy good deeds. Begin, and, Gilbert, – I have heard thou art somewhat careless – do not twist his words from his true meaning.'

"So – fear of death in the dark being upon him – Fulke began, and Gilbert, not knowing what his fate might be, wrote it word by word. I have heard many tales, but never heard I aught to match the tale of Fulke his black life, as Fulke told it hollowly, hanging in the shaft."

"Was it bad?" said Dan, awestruck.

"Beyond belief," Sir Richard answered. "None the less, there was that in it which forced even Gilbert to laugh. We three laughed till we ached. At one place his teeth so chattered that we could not well hear, and we reached him down a cup of wine. Then he warmed to it, and smoothly set out all his shifts, malices, and treacheries, his extreme boldnesses (he was desperate bold); his retreats, shufflings, and counterfeitings (he was also inconceivably a coward); his lack of gear and honour; his despair at their loss; his remedies, and well-coloured contrivances. Yes, he waved the filthy rags of his life before us, as though they had been some proud banner. When he ceased, we saw by torches that the tide stood at the corners of his mouth, and he breathed strongly through his nose.

"We had him out, and rubbed him; we wrapped him in a cloak, and gave him wine, and we leaned and looked upon him, the while he drank. He was shivering, but shameless.

"Of a sudden we heard Jehan at the stairway wake, but a boy pushed past him, and stood before us, the Hall-rushes in his hair, all slubbered with sleep. 'My father! My father! I dreamed of treachery,' he cried, and babbled thickly.

"'There is no treachery here,' said Fulke. 'Go!' and the boy turned, even then not fully awake, and Jehan led him by the hand to the Great Hall.

"'Thy only son!' said De Aquila. 'Why didst thou bring the child here?'

"'He is my heir. I dared not trust him to my brother,' said Fulke, and now he was ashamed. De Aquila said nothing, but sat weighing a wine-cup in his two hands thus. Anon, Fulke touched him on the knee.

"'Let the boy escape to Normandy,' said he, 'and do with me at thy pleasure. Yea, hang me tomorrow, with my letter to Robert round my neck, but let the boy go.'

"'Be still,' said De Aquila. 'I think for England.'

"So we waited what our Lord of Pevensey should devise; and the sweat ran down Fulke's forehead.

"At last said De Aquila: 'I am too old to judge, or to trust any man. I do not covet thy lands, as thou hast coveted mine; and whether thou art any better or any worse than any other black Angevin thief, it is for thy King to find out. Therefore, go back to thy King, Fulke.'

"'And thou wilt say nothing of what has passed?' said Fulke.

"'Why should I? Thy son will stay with me. If the King calls me again to leave Pevensey, which I must guard against England's enemies; if the King sends his men against me for a traitor; or if I hear that the King in his bed thinks any evil of me or my two knights, thy son will be hanged from out this window, Fulke.'"

"But it hadn't anything to do with his son," cried Una, startled.

"How could we have hanged Fulke?" said Sir Richard. "We needed him to make our peace with the King. He would have betrayed half England for the boy's sake. Of that we were sure."

"I don't understand," said Una. "But I think it was simply awful."

"So did not Fulke. He was well pleased."

"What? Because his son was going to be killed?"

"Nay. Because De Aquila had shown him how he might save the boy's life and his own lands and honours. 'I will do it,' he said. 'I swear I will do it. I will tell the King thou art no traitor, but the most excellent, valiant, and perfect of us all. Yes, I will save thee.'

"De Aquila looked still into the bottom of the cup, rolling the wine-dregs to and fro.

"'Ay,' he said. 'If I had a son, I would, I think, save him. But do not by any means tell me how thou wilt go about it.'

"'Nay, nay,' said Fulke, nodding his bald head wisely. 'That is my secret. But rest at ease, De Aquila, no hair of thy head nor rood of thy land shall be forfeited,' and he smiled like one planning great good deeds.

"'And henceforward,' said De Aquila, 'I counsel thee to serve one master, not two.'

"'What?' said Fulke. 'Can I work no more honest trading between the two sides these troublous times?'

"'Serve Robert or the King – England or Normandy,' said De Aquila. 'I care not which it is, but make thy choice here and now.'

"'The King, then,' said Fulke, 'for I see he is better served than Robert. Shall I swear it?'

"'No need,' said De Aquila, and he laid his hand on the parchments which Gilbert had written. 'It shall be some part of my Gilbert's penance to copy out the savoury tale of thy life, till we have made ten, twenty, an hundred, maybe, copies. How many cattle, think you, would the Bishop of Tours give for that tale? Or thy brother? Or the Monks of Blois? Minstrels will turn it into songs which thy own Saxon serfs shall sing behind their plough stilts, and men-at-arms riding through thy Norman towns. From here to Rome, Fulke, men will make very merry over that tale, and how Fulke told it, hanging in a well, like a drowned puppy. This shall be thy punishment, if ever I find thee double-dealing with thy King any more. Meantime, the parchments stay here with thy son. Him I will return to thee when thou hast made my peace with the King. The parchments never.'

Fulke hid his face and groaned.

"'Bones of the Saints!' said De Aquila, laughing. 'The pen cuts deep. I could never have fetched that grunt out of thee with any sword.'

"'But so long as I do not anger thee, my tale will be secret?' said Fulke.

"'Just so long. Does that comfort thee, Fulke?' said De Aquila.

"'What other comfort have ye left me?' he said, and of a

sudden he wept hopelessly like a child, dropping his face on his knees."

"Poor Fulke," said Una.

"I pitied him also," said Sir Richard.

"'After the spur, corn,' said De Aquila, and he threw Fulke three wedges of gold that he had taken from our little chest by the bedplace.

"'If I had known this,' said Fulke, catching his breath, 'I would never have lifted hand against Pevensey. Only lack of this yellow stuff has made me so unlucky in my dealings.'

"It was dawn then, and they stirred in the Great Hall below. We sent down Fulke's mail to be scoured, and when he rode away at noon under his own and the King's banner very splendid and stately did he show. He smoothed his long beard, and called his son to his stirrup and kissed him. De Aquila rode with him as far as the New Mill landward. We thought the night had been all a dream."

"But did he make it right with the King?" Dan asked. "About your not being traitors, I mean?"

Sir Richard smiled. "The King sent no second summons to Pevensey, nor did he ask why De Aquila had not obeyed the first. Yes, that was Fulke's work. I know not how he did it, but it was well and swiftly done."

"Then you didn't do anything to his son?" said Una.

"The boy? Oh, he was an imp! He turned the keep doors out of dortoirs while we had him. He sang foul songs, learned in the Barons' camps – poor fool; he set the hounds fighting in Hall; he lit the rushes to drive out, as he said, the fleas; he drew his dagger on Jehan, who threw him down the stairway for it; and he rode his horse through crops and among sheep. But when we had beaten him, and showed him wolf and deer, he followed us old men like a young, eager hound, and called us 'uncle'. His father came the summer's end to take him away, but the boy had no lust to go, because of the otter-hunting, and he stayed on till the fox-hunting. I gave him a bittern's claw to bring him good luck at shooting. An imp, if ever there was!"

"And what happened to Gilbert?" said Dan.

"Not even a whipping. De Aquila said he would sooner a clerk, however false, that knew the Manor roll than a fool, however true, that must be taught his work afresh. Moreover, after that night I think Gilbert loved as much as he feared De Aquila. At least he would not leave us not even when Vivian, the King's Clerk, would have made him Sacristan of Battle Abbey. A false fellow, but, in his fashion, bold."

"Did Robert ever land in Pevensey after all?" Dan went on.

"We guarded the coast too well while Henry was fighting his Barons; and three or four years later, when England had peace, Henry crossed to Normandy and showed his brother some work at Tenchebrai that cured Robert of fighting. Many of Henry's men sailed from Pevensey to that war. Fulke came, I remember, and we all four lay in the little chamber once again, and drank together. De Aquila was right. One should not judge men. Fulke was merry. Yes, always merry – with a catch in his breath."

"And what did you do afterwards?" said Una.

"We talked together of times past. That is all men can do when they grow old, little maid."

The bell for tea rang faintly across the meadows. Dan lay in the bows of the *Golden Hind;* Una in the stern, the book of verses open in her lap, was reading from "The Slave's Dream":

> "Again, in the mist and shadow of sleep,
> He saw his native land."

"I don't know when you began that," said Dan, sleepily.

On the middle thwart of the boat, beside Una's sunbonnet, lay an Oak leaf, an Ash leaf, and a Thorn leaf, that must have dropped down from the trees above; and the brook giggled as though it had just seen some joke.

THE RUNES ON WELAND'S SWORD

A Smith makes me
To betray my Man
In my first fight.

To gather Gold
At the world's end
I am sent.

The Gold I gather
Comes into England
Out of deep Water.

Like a shining Fish
Then it descends
Into deep Water.

It is not given
For goods or gear,
But for The Thing.

The Gold I gather
A King covets
For an ill use.

The Gold I gather
Is drawn up
Out of deep Water.

Like a shining Fish
Then it descends
Into deep Water.

It is not given
For goods or gear,
But for The Thing.

A Centurion of the Thirtieth

Cities and Thrones and Powers
  Stand in Time's eye,
Almost as long as flowers,
  Which daily die:
But, as new buds put forth
  To glad new men,
Out of the spent and unconsidered Earth
  The Cities rise again.

This season's Daffodil,
  She never hears
What change, what chance, what chill,
  Cut down last year's:
But with bold countenance,
  And knowledge small,
Esteems her seven days' continuance
  To be perpetual.

So Time that is o'er-kind
  To all that be,
Ordains us e'en as blind,
  As bold as she:
That in our very death,
  And burial sure,
Shadow to shadow, well persuaded, saith,
  "See how our works endure!"

Dan had come to grief over his Latin, and was kept in; so Una went alone to Far Wood. Dan's big catapult and the

lead bullets that Hobden had made for him were hidden in
an old hollow beech-stub on the west of the wood. They
had named the place out of the verse in *Lays of Ancient
Rome:*

> From lordly Volaterrae,
>> Where scowls the far-famed hold
> Piled by the hands of giants
>> For Godlike Kings of old.

They were the "Godlike Kings", and when old Hobden
piled some comfortable brushwood between the big wooden
knees of Volaterrae, they called him "Hands of Giants".

Una slipped through their private gap in the fence, and
sat still awhile, scowling as scowlily and lordlily as she
knew how; for Volaterrae is an important watch-tower that
juts out of Far Wood just as Far Wood juts out of the hillside. Pook's Hill lay below her and all the turns of the
brook as it wanders out of the Willingford Woods, between
hop-gardens, to old Hobden's cottage at the Forge. The
sou'-west wind (there is always a wind by Volaterrae) blew
from the bare ridge where Cherry Clack Windmill stands.

Now wind prowling through woods sounds like exciting
things going to happen, and that is why on blowy days you
stand up in Volaterrae and shout bits of the *Lays* to suit its
noises.

Una took Dan's catapult from its secret place, and made
ready to meet Lars Porsena's army stealing through the
wind-whitened aspens by the brook. A gust boomed up the
valley, and Una chanted sorrowfully:

> "Verbenna down to Ostia
>> Hath wasted all the plain:
> Astur hath stormed Janiculum,
>> And the stout guards are slain."

But the wind, not charging fair to the wood, started aside

and shook a single oak in Gleason's pasture. Here it made itself all small and crouched among the grasses, waving the tips of them as a cat waves the tip of her tail before she springs.

"Now welcome – welcome, Sextus," sang Una, loading the catapult –

> "Now welcome to thy home!
> Why dost thou stay, and turn away?
> Here lies the road to Rome."

She fired into the face of the lull, to wake up the cowardly wind, and heard a grunt from behind a thorn in the pasture.

"Oh, my Winkie!" she said aloud, and that was something she had picked up from Dan. "I b'lieve I've tickled up a Gleason cow."

"You little painted beast!" a voice cried. "I'll teach you to sling your masters!"

She looked down most cautiously, and saw a young man covered with hoopy bronze armour all glowing among the late broom. But what Una admired beyond all was his great bronze helmet with a red horse-tail that flicked in the wind. She could hear the long hairs rasp on his shimmery shoulder-plates.

"What does the Faun mean," he said, half aloud to himself, "by telling me that the Painted People have changed?" He caught sight of Una's yellow head. "Have you seen a painted lead-slinger?" he called.

"No-o," said Una. "But if you've seen a bullet – "

"Seen?" cried the man. "It passed within a hair's breadth of my ear."

"Well, that was me. I'm most awfully sorry."

"Didn't the Faun tell you I was coming?" He smiled.

"Not if you mean Puck. I thought you were a Gleason cow. I – I didn't know you were a – a – What are you?"

He laughed outright, showing a set of splendid teeth. His

face and eyes were dark, and his eyebrows met above his big nose in one bushy black bar.

"They call me Parnesius. I have been a Centurion of the Seventh Cohort of the Thirtieth Legion – the Ulpia Victrix. Did you sling that bullet?"

"I did. I was using Dan's catapult," said Una.

"Catapults!" said he. "I ought to know something about them. Show me!"

He leaped the rough fence with a rattle of spear, shield, and armour, and hoisted himself into Volaterrae as quickly as a shadow.

"A sling on a forked stick. *I* understand!" he cried, and pulled at the elastic. "But what wonderful beast yields this stretching leather?"

"It's laccy – elastic. You put the bullet into that loop, and then you pull hard."

The man pulled, and hit himself square on his thumbnail.

"Each to his own weapon," he said gravely, handing it back. "I am better with the bigger machine, little maiden. But it's a pretty toy. A wolf would laugh at it. Aren't you afraid of wolves?"

"There aren't any," said Una.

"Never believe it! A wolf's like a Winged Hat. He comes when he isn't expected. Don't they hunt wolves here?"

"We don't hunt," said Una, remembering what she had heard from grown-ups. "We preserve – pheasants. Do you know them?"

"I ought to," said the young man, smiling again, and he imitated the cry of the cock-pheasant so perfectly that a bird answered out of the wood.

"What a big painted clucking fool is a pheasant!" he said. "Just like some Romans."

"But you're a Roman yourself, aren't you?" said Una.

"Ye-es and no. I'm one of a good few thousands who have never seen Rome except in a picture. My people have

lived at Vectis for generations. Vectis – that island West
yonder that you can see from so far in clear weather."

"Do you mean the Isle of Wight? It lifts up just before
rain, and you see it from the Downs."

"Very likely. Our villa's on the south edge of the Island,
by the Broken Cliffs. Most of it is three hundred years old,
but the cow-stables, where our first ancestor lived, must be
a hundred years older. Oh, quite that, because the founder
of our family had his land given him by Agricola at the Set-
tlement. It's not a bad little place for its size. In springtime
violets grow down to the very beach. I've gathered sea-
weeds for myself and violets for my Mother many a time
with our old nurse."

"Was your nurse a – a Romaness too?"

"No, a Numidian. Gods be good to her! A dear, fat,
brown thing with a tongue like a cowbell. She was a free
woman. By the way, are you free, maiden?"

"Oh, quite," said Una. "At least, till tea-time; and in summer our governess doesn't say much if we're late."

The young man laughed again – a proper understanding
laugh.

"I see," said he. "That accounts for your being in the
wood. We hid among the cliffs."

"Did you have a governess, then?"

"Did we not? A Greek, too. She had a way of clutching
her dress when she hunted us among the gorse bushes that
made us laugh. Then she'd say she'd get us whipped. She
never did, though, bless her! Aglaia was a thorough sports-
woman, for all her learning."

"But what lessons did you do – when – when you were
little?"

"Ancient history, the Classics, arithmetic and so on," he
answered. "My sister and I were thickheads, but my two
brothers (I'm the middle one) liked those things, and, of
course, Mother was clever enough for any six. She was

nearly as tall as I am, and she looked like the new statue on the Western Road – the Demeter of the Baskets, you know. And funny! Roma Dea! How Mother could make us laugh!"

"What at?"

"Little jokes and sayings that every family has. Don't you know?"

"I know *we* have, but I didn't know other people had them too," said Una. "Tell me about all your family, please."

"Good families are very much alike. Mother would sit spinning of evenings while Aglaia read in her corner, and Father did accounts, and we four romped about the passages. When our noise grew too loud the Pater would say, 'Less tumult! Less tumult! Have you never heard of a Father's right over his children? He can slay them, my loves – slay them dead, and the Gods highly approve of the action!' Then Mother would prim up her dear mouth over the wheel and answer: 'H'm! I'm afraid there can't be much of the Roman Father about you!' Then the Pater would roll up his accounts, and say, 'I'll show you!' and then – then, he'd be worse than any of us!"

"Fathers can – if they like," said Una, her eyes dancing.

"Didn't I say all good families are very much the same?"

"What did you do in summer?" said Una. "Play about, like us?"

"Yes, and we visited our friends. There are no wolves in Vectis. We had many friends, and as many ponies as we wished."

"It must have been lovely," said Una. "I hope it lasted for ever."

"Not quite, little maid. When I was about sixteen or seventeen, the Father felt gouty, and we all went to the Waters."

"What waters?"

"At Aquae Sulis. Every one goes there. You ought to get your Father to take you some day."

"But where? I don't know," said Una.

The young man looked astonished for a moment. "Aquae Sulis," he repeated. "The best baths in Britain. Just as good, I'm told, as Rome. All the old gluttons sit in hot water, and talk scandal and politics. And the Generals come through the streets with their guards behind them; and the magistrates come in their chairs with their stiff guards behind them; and you meet fortune-tellers, and goldsmiths, and merchants, and philosophers, and feather-sellers, and ultra-Roman Britons, and ultra-British Romans, and tame tribesmen pretending to be civilized, and Jew lecturers, and – oh, everybody interesting. We young people, of course, took no interest in politics. We had not the gout. There were many of our age like us. We did not find life sad."

"But while we were enjoying ourselves without thinking, my sister met the son of a magistrate in the West and a year afterwards she was married to him. My young brother, who was always interested in plants and roots, met the First Doctor of a Legion from the City of the Legions, and he decided that he would be an Army doctor. I do not think it is a profession for a well-born man, but then – I'm not my brother. He went to Rome to study medicine, and now he's First Doctor of a Legion in Egypt – at Antinoé, I think, but I have not heard from him for some time.

"My eldest brother came across a Greek philosopher, and told my Father that he intended to settle down on the estate as a farmer and a philosopher. You see," – the young man's eyes twinkled – "his philosopher was a long-haired one!"

"I thought philosophers were bald," said Una.

"Not all. She was very pretty. I don't blame him. Nothing could have suited me better than my eldest brother's doing this, for I was only too keen to join the Army. I had always feared I should have to stay at home and look after the estate while my brother took *this.*"

He rapped on his great glistening shield that never seemed to be in his way.

"So we were well contented – we young people – and we rode back to Clausentum along the Wood Road very quietly. But when we reached home, Aglaia, our governess, saw what had come to us. I remember her at the door, the torch over her head, watching us climb the cliff path from the boat. 'Aie! Aie!' she said. 'Children you went away. Men and a woman you return!' Then she kissed Mother, and Mother wept. Thus our visit to the Waters settled our fates for each of us, maiden."

He rose to his feet and listened, leaning on the shield-rim.

"I think that's Dan – my brother," said Una.

"Yes; and the Faun is with him," he replied, as Dan with Puck stumbled through the copse.

"We should have come sooner," Puck called, "but the beauties of your native tongue, O Parnesius, have enthralled this young citizen."

Parnesius looked bewildered, even when Una explained.

"Dan said the plural of 'dominus' was 'dominoes', and when Miss Blake said it wasn't he said he supposed it was 'backgammon', and so he had to write it out twice for cheek, you know."

Dan had climbed into Volaterrae, hot and panting.

"I've run nearly all the way," he gasped, "and then Puck met me. How do you do, sir?"

"I am in good health," Parnesius answered. "See! I have tried to bend the bow of Ulysses, but – " He held up his thumb.

"I'm sorry. You must have pulled off too soon," said Dan. "But Puck said you were telling Una a story."

"Continue, O Parnesius," said Puck, who had perched himself on a dead branch above them. "I will be chorus. Has he puzzled you much, Una?"

"Not a bit, except – I didn't know where Ak – Ak something was," she answered.

"Oh, Aquae Sulis. That's Bath, where the buns come from. Let the hero tell his own tale."

Parnesius pretended to thrust his spear at Puck's legs, but Puck reached down, caught at the horse-tail plume, and pulled off the tall helmet.

"Thanks, jester," said Parnesius, shaking his curly dark head. "That is cooler. Now hang it up for me . . ."

"I was telling your sister how I joined the Army," he said to Dan.

"Did you have to pass an Exam?" Dan asked eagerly.

"No. I went to my Father, and said I should like to enter the Dacian Horse (I had seen some at Aquae Sulis); but he said I had better begin service in a regular Legion from Rome. Now, like many of our youngsters, I was not too fond of anything Roman. The Roman-born officers and magistrates looked down on us British-born as though we were barbarians. I told my Father so."

"'I know they do,' he said; 'but remember, after all, we are the people of the Old Stock, and our duty is to the Empire.'

"'To which Empire?' I asked. 'We split the Eagle before I was born.'

"'What thieves' talk is that?' said my Father. He hated slang.

"'Well, sir,' I said, 'we've one Emperor in Rome, and I don't know how many Emperors the outlying Provinces have set up from time to time. Which am I to follow?'

"'Gratian,' said he. 'At least he's a sportsman.'

"'He's all that,' I said. 'Hasn't he turned himself into a raw-beef-eating Scythian?'

"'Where did you hear of it?' said the Pater.

"'At Aquae Sulis,' I said. It was perfectly true. This precious Emperor Gratian of ours had a bodyguard of fur-cloaked Scythians, and he was so crazy about them that he dressed like them. In Rome of all places in the world! It was as bad as if my own Father had painted himself blue!

"'No matter for the clothes,' said the Pater. 'They are

only the fringe of the trouble. It began before your time or mine. Rome has forsaken her Gods, and must be punished. The great war with the Painted People broke out in the very year the temples of our Gods were destroyed. We beat the Painted People in the very year our temples were rebuilt. Go back further still.' . . . He went back to the time of Diocletian; and to listen to him you would have thought Eternal Rome herself was on the edge of destruction, just because a few people had become a little large-minded.

"*I* knew nothing about it. Aglaia never taught us the history of our own country. She was so full of her ancient Greeks.

"'There is no hope for Rome,' said the Pater, at last. 'She has forsaken her Gods, but if the Gods forgive us here, we may save Britain. To do that, we must keep the Painted People back. Therefore, I tell you, Parnesius, as a Father, that if your heart is set on service, your place is among men on the Wall – and not with women among the cities.'"

"What Wall?" asked Dan and Una at once.

"Father meant the one we call Hadrian's Wall. I'll tell you about it later. It was built long ago, across North Britain, to keep out the Painted People – Picts, you call them. Father had fought in the great Pict War that lasted more than twenty years, and he knew what fighting meant. Theodosius, one of our great Generals, had chased the little beasts back far into the North before I was born. Down at Vectis, of course, we never troubled our heads about them. But when my Father spoke as he did, I kissed his hand, and waited for orders. We British born Romans know what is due to our parents."

"If I kissed my Father's hand, he'd laugh," said Dan.

"Customs change; but if you do not obey your Father, the Gods remember it. You may be quite sure of *that*."

"After our talk, seeing I was in earnest, the Pater sent me over to Clausentum to learn my foot-drill in a barrack full of foreign Auxiliaries – as unwashed and unshaved a mob of mixed barbarians as ever scrubbed a breastplate. It was your stick in their stomachs and your shield in their faces to push them into any sort of formation. When I had learned my work the Instructor gave me a handful – and they were a handful! – of Gauls and Iberians to polish up till they were sent to their stations up-country. I did my best, and one night a villa in the suburbs caught fire, and I had my handful out and at work before any of the other troops. I noticed a quiet-looking man on the lawn, leaning on a stick. He watched us passing buckets from the pond, and at last he said to me: 'Who are you?'

"'A probationer, waiting for a command,' I answered. *I* didn't know who he was from Deucalion!

"'Born in Britain?' he said.

"'Yes, if you were born in Spain,' I said, for he neighed his words like an Iberian mule.

"'And what might you call yourself when you are at home?' he said, laughing.

"'That depends,' I answered; 'sometimes one thing and sometimes another. But now I'm busy.'

"He said no more till we had saved the family Gods (they were respectable householders), and then he grunted across the laurels: 'Listen, young sometimes-one-thing-and-sometimes-another. In future call yourself Centurion of the Seventh Cohort of the Thirtieth, the Ulpia Victrix. That will help me to remember you. Your Father and a few other people call me Maximus.'

"He tossed me the polished stick he was leaning on, and went away. You might have knocked me down with it!"

"Who was he?" said Dan.

"Maximus himself, our great General! *The* General of Britain who had been Theodosius's right hand in the Pict War! Not only had he given me my Centurion's stick direct, but three steps in a good Legion as well! A new man generally begins in the Tenth Cohort of his Legion, and works up."

"And were you pleased?" said Una.

"Very. I thought Maximus had chosen me for my good looks and fine style in marching, but, when I went home, – the Pater told me he had served under Maximus in the great Pict War, and had asked him to befriend me."

"A child you were!" said Puck, from above.

"I was," said Parnesius. "Don't begrudge it me, Faun. Afterwards – the Gods know I put aside the games!" And Puck nodded, brown chin on brown hand, his big eyes still.

"The night before I left we sacrificed to our ancestors the usual little Home Sacrifice – but I never prayed so earnestly to all the Good Shades, and then I went with my Father by boat to Regnum, and across the chalk eastwards to Anderida yonder."

"Regnum? Anderida?" The children turned their faces to Puck.

"Regnum's Chichester," he said, pointing towards Cherry Clack, "and" – he threw his arm South behind him – "Anderida's Pevensey."

"Pevensey again?" said Dan. "Where Weland landed?"

"Weland and a few others," said Puck. "Pevensey isn't young – even compared to me!"

"The headquarters of the Thirtieth lay at Anderida in summer, but my own Cohort, the Seventh, was on the Wall up North. Maximus was inspecting Auxiliaries – the Abulci, I think – at Anderida, and we stayed with him, for he and my Father were very old friends. I was only there ten days when I was ordered to go up with thirty men to my Cohort." He laughed merrily. "A man never forgets his first march. I was happier than any Emperor when I led my handful through the North Gate of the Camp, and we saluted the guard and the Altar of Victory there."

"How? How?" said Dan and Una.

Parnesius smiled, and stood up, flashing in his armour.

"So!" said he; and he moved slowly through the beautiful movements of the Roman Salute, that ends with a hollow clang of the shield coming into its place between the shoulders.

"Hai!" said Puck. "That sets one thinking!"

"We went out fully armed," said Parnesius, sitting down; "but as soon as the road entered the Great Forest, my men expected the pack-horses to hang their shields on. 'No!' I said; 'you can dress like women in Anderida, but while you're with me you will carry your own weapons and armour.'

"'But it's hot,' said one of them, 'and we haven't a doctor. Suppose we get sunstroke, or a fever?'

"'Then die,' I said, 'and a good riddance to Rome! Up shield – up spears, and tighten your foot-wear!'

"'Don't think yourself Emperor of Britain already,' a fellow shouted. I knocked him over with the butt of my spear, and explained to these Roman-born Romans that, if there were any further trouble, we should go on with one man short. And, by the Light of the Sun, I meant it too! My raw Gauls at Clausentum had never treated me so.

"Then, quietly as a cloud, Maximus rode out of the fern (my Father behind him), and reined up across the road. He wore the Purple, as though he were already Emperor; his leggings were of white buckskin laced with gold.

"My men dropped like – like partridges.

"He said nothing for some time, only looked, with his eyes puckered. Then he crooked his forefinger, and my men walked – crawled, I mean – to one side.

"'Stand in the sun, children,' he said, and they formed up on the hard road.

"'What would you have done,' he said to me, 'if I had not been here?'

"'I should have killed that man,' I answered.

"'Kill him now' he said. 'He will not move a limb.'

"'No,' I said. 'You've taken my men out of my command. I should only be your butcher if I killed him now.' Do you see what I meant?" Parnesius turned to Dan.

"Yes," said Dan. "It wouldn't have been fair, somehow."

"That was what I thought," said Parnesius. "But Maximus frowned. 'You'll never be an Emperor,' he said. 'Not even a General will you be.'

"I was silent, but my Father seemed pleased."

"'I came here to see the last of you,' he said.

"'You have seen it,' said Maximus. 'I shall never need your son any more. He will live and he will die an officer of a Legion – and he might have been Prefect of one of my Provinces. Now eat and drink with us,' he said. 'Your men will wait till you have finished.'

"My miserable thirty stood like wine-skins glistening in the hot sun, and Maximus led us to where his people had set a meal. Himself he mixed the wine.

"'A year from now,' he said, 'you will remember that you have sat with the Emperor of Britain – and Gaul.'

"'Yes,' said the Pater, 'you can drive two mules – Gaul and Britain.'

"'Five years hence you will remember that you have drunk' – he passed me the cup and there was blue borage in it – 'with the Emperor of Rome!'

"'No; you can't drive three mules. They will tear you in pieces,' said my Father.

"'And you on the Wall, among the heather, will weep because your notion of justice was more to you than the favour of the Emperor of Rome.'

"I sat quite still. One does not answer a General who wears the Purple."

"'I am not angry with you,' he went on; 'I owe too much to your Father – '

"'You owe me nothing but advice that you never took,' said the Pater.

"' – to be unjust to any of your family. Indeed, I say you may make a good Tribune, but, so far as I am concerned, on the Wall you will live, and on the Wall you will die,' said Maximus.

"'Very like,' said my Father. 'But we shall have the Picts *and* their friends breaking through before long. You cannot move all troops out of Britain to make you Emperor, and expect the North to sit quiet.'

"'I follow my destiny,' said Maximus.

"'Follow it, then,' said my Father, pulling up a fern root; 'and die as Theodosius died.'

"'Ah!' said Maximus. 'My old General was killed because he served the Empire too well. *I* may be killed, but not for that reason,' and he smiled a little pale grey smile that made my blood run cold.

"'Then I had better follow my destiny,' I said, 'and take my men to the Wall.'

"He looked at me a long time, and bowed his head slanting like a Spaniard. 'Follow it, boy,' he said. That was all. I was only too glad to get away, though I had many messages for home. I found my men standing as they had been put – they had not even shifted their feet in the dust, and off I marched, still feeling that terrific smile like an east wind up my back. I never halted them till sunset, and" – he turned about and looked at Pook's Hill below him – "then I halted yonder." He pointed to the broken, bracken-covered shoulder of the Forge Hill behind old Hobden's cottage.

"There? Why, that's only the old Forge – where they made iron once," said Dan.

"Very good stuff it was too," said Parnesius calmly. "We mended three shoulder-straps here and had a spear-head riveted. The Forge was rented from the Government by a one-eyed smith from Carthage. I remember we called him Cyclops. He sold me a beaver-skin rug for my sister's room."

"But it couldn't have been here," Dan insisted.

"But it was! From the Altar of Victory at Anderida to the First Forge in the Forest here is twelve miles seven hundred paces. It is all in the Road Book. A man doesn't forget his first march. I think I could tell you every station between this and – " He leaned forward, but his eye was caught by the setting sun.

It had come down to the top of Cherry Clack Hill, and the light poured in between the tree trunks so that you could see red and gold and black deep into the heart of Far Wood; and Parnesius in his armour shone as though he had been afire.

"Wait!" he said, lifting a hand, and the sunlight jinked on his glass bracelet. "Wait! I pray to Mithras!"

He rose and stretched his arms westward, with deep, splendid-sounding words.

Then Puck began to sing too, in a voice like bells tolling, and as he sang he slipped from Volaterrae to the ground, and beckoned the children to follow. They obeyed; it seemed as though the voices were pushing them along; and through the goldy-brown light on the beech leaves they walked, while Puck between them chanted something like this:

> *"Cur mundus militat sub vana gloria*
> *Cujus prospentas est transitoria?*
> *Tam cito labitur ejus potentia*
> *Quam vasa figuli quae sunt fragilia."*

They found themselves at the little locked gates of the wood.

> *"Quo Caesar abiit celsus imperio?*
> *Vel Dives splendidus totus in prandio?*
> *Dic ubi Tullius – "*

Still singing, he took Dan's hand and wheeled him round

to face Una as she came out of the gate. It shut behind her, at the same time as Puck threw the memory-magicking Oak, Ash and Thorn leaves over their heads.

"Well, you *are* jolly late," said Una. "Couldn't you get away before?"

"I did," said Dan. "I got away in lots of time, but – but I didn't know it was so late. Where've you been?"

"In Volaterrae – waiting for you."

"Sorry," said Dan. "It was all that beastly Latin."

A BRITISH-ROMAN SONG
(AD 406)

My father's father saw it not,
*   And I, belike, shall never come*
To look on that so-holy spot –
*   The very Rome –*

Crowned by all Time, all Art, all Might,
*   The equal work of Gods and Man,*
City beneath whose oldest height –
*   The Race began!*

Soon to send forth again a brood,
*   Unshakeable, we pray, that clings*
To Rome's thrice-hammered hardihood –
*   In arduous things.*

Strong heart with triple armour bound,
*   Beat strongly, for Thy life-blood runs,*
Age after Age, the Empire round
*   In us Thy Sons,*

Who, distant from the Seven Hills,
*   Loving and serving much, require*
Thee – Thee to guard 'gainst home-born ills
*   The Imperial Fire!*

On the Great Wall

"When I left Rome for Lalage's sake
  By the Legions' Road to Rimini,
She vowed her heart was mine to take
  With me and my shield to Rimini —
  (Till the Eagles flew from Rimini!)
    And I've tramped Britain, and I've tramped Gaul,
    And the Pontic shore where the snow-flakes fall
  As white as the neck of Lalage —
  (As cold as the heart of Lalage!)
    And I've lost Britain, and I've lost Gaul,"

(the voice seemed very cheerful about it),

  "And I've lost Rome, and, worst of all,
    I've lost Lalage!"

They were standing by the gate to Far Wood when they heard this song. Without a word they hurried to their private gap and wriggled through the hedge almost atop of a jay that was feeding from Puck's hand.

"Gently!" said Puck. "What are you looking for?"

"Parnesius, of course," Dan answered. "We've only just remembered yesterday. It isn't fair."

Puck chuckled as he rose. "I'm sorry, but children who spend the afternoon with me and a Roman Centurion need a little settling dose of Magic before they go to tea with their governess. Ohé, Parnesius!" he called.

"Here, Faun!" came the answer from Volaterrae. They could see the shimmer of bronze armour in the beech crotch, and the friendly flash of the great shield uplifted.

"I have driven out the Britons." Parnesius laughed like a boy. "I occupy their high forts. But Rome is merciful! You may come up." And up they three all scrambled.

"What was the song you were singing just now?" said Una, as soon as she had settled herself.

"That? Oh, *Rimini*. It's one of the tunes that are always being born somewhere in the Empire. They run like a pestilence for six months or a year, till another one pleases the Legions, and then they march to *that*."

"Tell them about the marching, Parnesius. Few people nowadays walk from end to end of this country," said Puck.

"The greater their loss. I know nothing better than the Long March when your feet are hardened. You begin after the mists have risen, and you end, perhaps, an hour after sundown."

"And what do you have to eat?" Dan asked promptly.

"Fat bacon, beans, and bread, and whatever wine happens to be in the rest-houses. But soldiers are born grumblers. Their very first day out, my men complained of our water-ground British corn. They said it wasn't so filling as the rough stuff that is ground in the Roman ox-mills. However, they had to fetch and eat it."

"Fetch it? Where from?" said Una.

"From that newly invented water-mill below the Forge."

"That's Forge Mill – *our* Mill!" Una looked at Puck.

"Yes; yours," Puck put in. "How old did you think it was?"

"I don't know. Didn't Sir Richard Dalyngridge talk about it?"

"He did, and it was old in his day," Puck answered. "Hundreds of years old."

"It was new in mine," said Parnesius. "My men looked at the flour in their helmets as though it had been a nest of adders. They did it to try my patience. But I – addressed them, and we became friends. To tell the truth, they taught me the Roman Step. You see, I'd only served with quick-marching Auxiliaries. A Legion's pace is altogether different. It is a long, slow stride, that never varies from sunrise to sunset. 'Rome's Race – Rome's Pace,' as the proverb says. Twenty-four miles in eight hours, neither more nor less. Head and spear up, shield on your back, cuirass collar open one hand's-breadth – and that's how you take the Eagles through Britain."

"And did you meet any adventures?" said Dan.

"There are no adventures South the Wall," said Parnesius. "The worst thing that happened me was having to appear before a magistrate up North, where a wandering philosopher had jeered at the Eagles. I was able to show that the old man had deliberately blocked our road; and the magistrate told him, out of his own Book, I believe, that, whatever his Gods might be, he should pay proper respect to Caesar."

"What did you do?" said Dan.

"Went on. Why should *I* care for such things, my business being to reach my station? It took me twenty days."

"Of course, the farther North you go the emptier are the roads. At last you fetch clear of the forests and climb bare hills, where wolves howl in the ruins of our cities that have been. No more pretty girls; no more jolly magistrates who knew your Father when he was young, and invite you to stay with them; no news at the temples and way-stations except bad news of wild beasts. There's where you meet hunters, and trappers for the Circuses, prodding along chained bears and muzzled wolves. Your pony shies at them, and your men laugh.

"The houses change from gardened villas to shut forts with watch-towers of grey stone, and great stone-walled sheepfolds, guarded by armed Britons of the North Shore. In the naked hills beyond the naked houses, where the shadows of the clouds play like cavalry charging, you see puffs of black smoke from the mines. The hard road goes on and on – and the wind sings through your helmet-plume – past altars to Legions and Generals forgotten, and broken statues of Gods and Heroes, and thousands of graves where the mountain foxes and hares peep at you. Red-hot in summer, freezing in winter, is that big, purple heather country of broken stone.

"Just when you think you are at the world's end, you see a smoke from East to West as far as the eye can turn, and then, under it, also as far as the eye can stretch, houses and temples, shops and theatres, barracks and granaries, trickling along like dice behind – always behind – one long, low, rising and falling, and hiding and showing line of towers. And that is the Wall!"

"Ah!" said the children, taking breath.

"You may well," said Parnesius. "Old men who have followed the Eagles since boyhood say nothing in the Empire is more wonderful than first sight of the Wall!"

"Is it just *a* Wall? Like the one round the kitchen-garden?" said Dan.

"No, no! It is *the* Wall. Along the top are towers with guard-houses, small towers, between. Even on the narrowest part of it three men with shields can walk abreast, from guard-house to guard-house. A little curtain wall, no higher than a man's neck, runs along the top of the thick wall, so that from a distance you see the helmets of the sentries sliding back and forth like beads. Thirty feet high is the Wall, and on the Picts' side, the North, is a ditch, strewn with blades of old swords and spear-heads set in wood, and tyres of wheels joined by chains. The Little People come there to steal iron for their arrow-heads.

"But the Wall itself is not more wonderful than the town behind it. Long ago there were great ramparts and ditches on the South side, and no one was allowed to build there. Now the ramparts are partly pulled down and built over, from end to end of the Wall; making a thin town eighty miles long. Think of it! One roaring, rioting, cock-fighting, wolf-baiting, horse-racing town, from Ituna on the West to Segedunum on the cold eastern beach! On one side heather, woods and ruins where Picts hide, and on the other, a vast town – long like a snake, and wicked like a snake. Yes, a snake basking beside a warm wall!

"My Cohort, I was told, lay at Hunno, where the Great North Road runs through the Wall into the Province of Valentia." Parnesius laughed scornfully. "The Province of Valentia! We followed the road, therefore, into Hunno town, and stood astonished. The place was a fair – a fair of peoples from every corner of the Empire. Some were racing horses: some sat in wine-shops: some watched dogs baiting bears, and many gathered in a ditch to see cocks fight. A boy not much older than myself, but I could see he was an officer, reined up before me and asked what I wanted.

"'My station,' I said, and showed him my shield." Parnesius held up his broad shield with its three X's like letters on a beer-cask.

"'Lucky omen!' said he. 'Your Cohort's the next tower to us, but they're all at the cock-fight. This is a happy place. Come and wet the Eagles.' He meant to offer me a drink.

"'When I've handed over my men,' I said. I felt angry and ashamed.

"'Oh, you'll soon outgrow that sort of nonsense,' he answered. 'But don't let me interfere with your hopes. Go on to the Statue of Roma Dea. You can't miss it. The main road into Valentia!' and he laughed and rode off. I could see the statue not a quarter of a mile away, and there I went. At some time or other the Great North Road ran under it into Valentia; but the far end had been blocked up because of the Picts, and on the plaster a man had scratched, 'Finish!' It was like marching into a cave. We grounded spears together, my little thirty, and it echoed in the barrel of the arch, but none came. There was a door at one side painted with our number. We prowled in, and I found a cook asleep, and ordered him to give us food. Then I climbed to the top of the Wall, and looked out over the Pict country, and I – thought," said Parnesius. "The bricked-up arch with 'Finish!' on the plaster was what shook me, for I was not much more than a boy."

"What a shame!" said Una. "But did you feel happy after you'd had a good – " Dan stopped her with a nudge.

"Happy?" said Parnesius. "When the men of the Cohort I was to command came back unhelmeted from the cock-fight, their birds under their arms, and asked me who I was? No, I was not happy; but I made my new Cohort unhappy too . . . I wrote my Mother I was happy, but, oh, my friends" – he stretched arms over bare knees "I would not wish my worst enemy to suffer as I suffered through my first months on the Wall. Remember this: among the officers was scarcely one, except myself (and I thought I had lost the fa-vour of Maximus, my General), scarcely one who had not done something of wrong or folly. Either he had killed a man, or taken money, or insulted the magistrates, or blas-phemed the Gods, and so had been sent to the Wall as a hiding-place from shame or fear. And the men were as the officers. Remember, also, that the Wall was manned by every breed and race in the Empire. No two towers spoke the same tongue, or worshipped the same Gods. In one thing only we were all equal. No matter what arms we had used before we came to the Wall, *on* the Wall we were all archers, like the Scythians. The Pict cannot run away from the arrow, or crawl under it. He is a bowman himself. *He* knows!"

"I suppose you were fighting Picts all the time," said Dan.

"Picts seldom fight. I never saw a fighting Pict for half a year. The tame Picts told us they had all gone North."

"What is a tame Pict?" said Dan.

"A Pict – there were many such – who speaks a few words of our tongue, and slips across the Wall to sell ponies and wolf-hounds. Without a horse and a dog, *and* a friend, man would perish. The Gods gave me all three, and there is no gift like friendship. Remember this" – Parnesius turned to Dan – "when you become a young man. For your fate will turn on the first true friend you make."

"He means," said Puck, grinning, "that if you try to make yourself a decent chap when you're young, you'll make rather decent friends when you grow up. If you're a beast, you'll have beastly friends. Listen to the Pious Parnesius on Friendship!"

"I am not pious," Parnesius answered, "but I know what goodness means; and my friend, though he was without hope, was ten thousand times better than I. Stop laughing, Faun!"

"Oh, Youth Eternal and All-believing," cried Puck, as he rocked on the branch above. "Tell them about your Pertinax."

"He was that friend the Gods sent me – the boy who spoke to me when I first came. Little older than myself, commanding the Augusta Victoria Cohort on the tower next to us and the Numidians. In virtue he was far my superior."

"Then why was he on the Wall?" Una asked, quickly. "They'd all done something bad. You said so yourself."

"He was the nephew, his father had died, of a great rich man in Gaul who was not always kind to his mother. When Pertinax grew up, he discovered this, and so his uncle shipped him off, by trickery and force, to the Wall. We came to know each other at a ceremony in our Temple – in the dark. It was the Bull-Killing," Parnesius explained to Puck.

"*I* see," said Puck, and turned to the children. "That's something you wouldn't quite understand. Parnesius means he met Pertinax in church."

"Yes – in the Cave we first met, and we were both raised to the Degree of Gryphons together." Parnesius lifted his hand towards his neck for an instant. "He had been on the Wall two years, and knew the Picts well. He taught me first how to take Heather."

"What's that?" said Dan.

"Going out hunting in the Pict country with a tame Pict. You are quite safe so long as you are his guest, and wear a sprig of heather where it can be seen. If you went alone you would surely be killed, if you were not smothered first in the bogs. Only the Picts know their way about those black and hidden bogs. Old Allo, the one-eyed, withered little Pict from whom we bought our ponies, was our special friend. At first we went only to escape from the terrible town, and to talk together about our homes. Then he showed us how to hunt wolves and those great red deer with horns like Jewish candlesticks. The Roman-born officers rather looked down on us for doing this, but we preferred the heather to their amusements. Believe me," Parnesius turned again to Dan, "a boy is safe from all things that really harm when he is astride a pony or after a deer. Do you remember, O Faun," – he turned to Puck – "the little altar I built to the Sylvan Pan by the pine-forest beyond the brook?"

"Which? The stone one with the line from Xenophon?" said Puck, in quite a new voice.

"No! What do *I* know of Xenophon? That was Pertinax after he had shot his first mountain-hare with an arrow by chance! Mine I made of round pebbles in memory of my first bear. It took me one happy day to build." Parnesius faced the children quickly.

"And that was how we lived on the Wall for two years – a little scuffling with the Picts, and a great deal of hunting with old Allo in the Pict country. He called us his children sometimes, and we were fond of him and his barbarians,

though we never let them paint us Pict-fashion. The marks
endure till you die."

"How's it done?" said Dan. "Anything like tattooing?"

"They prick the skin till the blood runs, and rub in col-
oured juices. Allo was painted blue, green, and red from his
forehead to his ankles. He said it was part of his religion.
He told us about his religion (Pertinax was always interested in such things), and as we came to know him well, he
told us what was happening in Britain behind the Wall.
Many things took place behind us in those days. And by the
Light of the Sun," said Parnesius, earnestly, "there was not
much that those little people did not know! He told me
when Maximus crossed over to Gaul, after he had made
himself Emperor of Britain, and what troops and emigrants
he had taken with him. We did not get the news on the Wall
till fifteen days later. He told me what troops Maximus was
taking out of Britain every month to help him to conquer
Gaul; and I always found the numbers were as he said.
Wonderful! And I tell another strange thing!"

He jointed his hands across his knees, and leaned his
head on the curve of the shield behind him.

"Late in the summer, when the first frosts begin and the
Picts kill their bees, we three rode out after wolf with some
new hounds. Rutilianus, our General, had given us ten
days' leave, and we had pushed beyond the Second Wall –
beyond the Province of Valentia – into the higher hills,
where there are not even any of old Rome's ruins. We killed
a she-wolf before noon, and while Allo was skinning her he
looked up and said to me, 'When you are Captain of the
Wall, my child, you won't be able to do this any more!'

"I might as well have been made Prefect of Lower Gaul,
so I laughed and said, 'Wait till I am Captain.' 'No, don't
wait,' said Allo. 'Take my advice and go home both of
you.' 'We have no homes,' said Pertinax. 'You know that as
well as we do. We're finished men – thumbs down against

both of us. Only men without hope would risk their necks
on your ponies.' The old man laughed one of those short
Pict laughs – like a fox barking on a frosty night. 'I'm fond
of you two,' he said. 'Besides, I've taught you what little
you know about hunting. Take my advice and go home.'

"'We can't,' I said. 'I'm out of favour with my General,
for one thing; and for another, Pertinax has an uncle.'

"'I don't know about his uncle,' said Allo, 'but the trouble with you, Parnesius, is that your General thinks well of
you.'

"'Roma Dea!' said Pertinax, sitting up. 'What can you
guess what Maximus thinks, you old horse-coper?'

"Just then (you know how near the brutes creep when one
is eating?) a great dog-wolf jumped out behind us, and
away our rested hounds tore after him, with us at their tails.
He ran us far out of any country we'd ever heard of, straight
as an arrow till sunset, towards the sunset. We came at last
to long capes stretching into winding waters, and on a grey
beach below us we saw ships drawn up. Forty-seven we
counted – not Roman galleys but the raven-winged ships
from the North where Rome does not rule. Men moved in
the ships, and the sun flashed on their helmets – winged
helmets of the red-haired men from the North where Rome
does not rule. We watched, and we counted, and we wondered, for though we had heard rumours concerning these
Winged Hats, as the Picts called them, never before had we
looked upon them.

"'Come away! come away!' said Allo. 'My Heather
won't protect you here. We shall all be killed!' His legs
trembled like his voice. Back we went – back across the
heather under the moon, till it was nearly morning, and our
poor beasts stumbled on some ruins.

"When we woke, very stiff and cold, Allo was mixing the
meal and water. One does not light fires in the Pict country
except near a village. The little men are always signalling

to each other with smokes, and a strange smoke brings them out buzzing like bees. They can sting, too!"

"'What we saw last night was a trading-station,' said Allo. 'Nothing but a trading-station.'

"'I do not like lies on an empty stomach,' said Pertinax. 'I suppose' (he had eyes like an eagle's) – 'I suppose *that* is a trading-station also?" He pointed to a smoke far off on a hill top, ascending in what we call the Picts' Call: – Puff – double-puff: double-puff – puff! They make it by raising and dropping a wet hide on a fire.

"'No,' said Allo, pushing the platter back into the bag. 'That is for you and me. Your fate is fixed. Come.'

"We came. When one takes Heather, one must obey one's Pict – but that wretched smoke was twenty miles distant, well over on the East coast, and the day was as hot as a bath.

"'Whatever happens,' said Allo, while our ponies grunted along, 'I want you to remember me.'

"'I shall not forget,' said Pertinax. 'You have cheated me out of my breakfast.'

"'What is a handful of crushed oats to a Roman?' he said. Then he laughed his laugh that was not a laugh.

"'What would *you* do if *you* were a handful of oats being crushed between the upper and lower stones of a mill?'

"'I'm Pertinax, not a riddle-guesser,' said Pertinax.

"'You're a fool,' said Allo. 'Your Gods and my Gods are threatened by strange Gods, and all you can do is to laugh.'

"'Threatened men live long,' I said.

"'I pray the Gods that may be true,' he said. 'But I ask you again not to forget me.'

"We climbed the last hot hill and looked out on the eastern sea, three or four miles off. There was a small sailing- galley of the North Gaul pattern at anchor, her landing plank down and her sail half up; and below us, alone in a hollow, holding his pony, sat Maximus, Emperor of Britain!

He was dressed like a hunter, and he leaned on his little stick; but I knew that back as far as I could see it, and I told Pertinax.

"'You're madder than Allo!' he said. 'It must be the sun!'

"Maximus never stirred till we stood before him. Then he looked me up and down, and said: 'Hungry again? It seems to be my destiny to feed you whenever we meet. I have food here. Allo shall cook it.'

"'No,' said Allo. 'A Prince in his own land does not wait on wandering Emperors. I feed my two children without asking your leave.' He began to blow up the ashes.

"'I was wrong,' said Pertinax. 'We are all mad. Speak up, O Madman called Emperor!'

"Maximus smiled his terrible tight-lipped smile, but two years on the Wall do not make a man afraid of mere looks. So I was not afraid.

"'I meant you, Parnesius, to live and die a Centurion of the Wall,' said Maximus. 'But it seems from these,' – he fumbled in his breast – 'you can think as well as draw.' He pulled out a roll of letters I had written to my people, full of drawings of Picts, and bears, and men I had met on the Wall. Mother and my sister always liked my pictures.

"He handed me one that I had called 'Maximus's Soldiers'. It showed a row of fat wine-skins, and our old Doctor of the Hunno hospital snuffing at them. Each time that Maximus had taken troops out of Britain to help him to conquer Gaul, he used to send the garrisons more wine – to keep them quiet, I suppose. On the Wall, we always called a wine-skin a 'Maximus'. Oh, yes; and I had drawn them in Imperial helmets.

"'Not long since,' he went on, 'men's names were sent up to Caesar for smaller jokes than this.'

"'True, Caesar,' said Pertinax; 'but you forget that was before I, your friend's friend, became such a good spear-thrower.'

"He did not actually point his hunting-spear at Maximus, but balanced it on his palm – so!

"'I was speaking of time past,' said Maximus, never fluttering an eyelid. 'Nowadays one is only too pleased to find boys who can think for themselves, *and* their friends.' He nodded at Pertinax. 'Your Father lent me the letters, Parnesius, so you run no risk from me.'

"'None whatever,' said Pertinax, and rubbed the spear point on his sleeve.

"'I have been forced to reduce the garrisons in Britain, because I need troops in Gaul. Now I come to take troops from the Wall itself,' said he.

"'I wish you joy of us,' said Pertinax. 'We're the last sweepings of the Empire – the men without hope. Myself, I'd sooner trust condemned criminals.'

"'You think so?' he said, quite seriously. 'But it will only be till I win Gaul. One must always risk one's life, or one's soul, or one's peace – or some little thing.'

"Allo passed round the fire with the sizzling deer's meat. He served us two first.

"'Ah!' said Maximus, waiting his turn. 'I perceive you are in your own country. Well, you deserve it. They tell me you have quite a following among the Picts, Parnesius.'

"'I have hunted with them,' I said. 'Maybe I have a few friends among the heather.'

"'He is the only armoured man of you all who understands us,' said Allo, and he began a long speech about our virtues, and how we had saved one of his grand-children from a wolf the year before."

"Had you?" said Una.

"Yes; but that was neither here nor there. The little green man orated like a – like Cicero. He made us out to be magnificent fellows. Maximus never took his eyes off our faces.

"'Enough,' he said. 'I have heard Allo on you. I wish to hear you on the Picts.'"

"I told him as much as I knew, and Pertinax helped me out. There is never harm in a Pict if you but take the trouble to find out what he wants. Their real grievance against us came from our burning their heather. The whole garrison of the Wall moved out twice a year, and solemnly burned the heather for ten miles North. Rutilianus, our General, called it clearing the country. The Picts, of course, scampered away, and all we did was to destroy their bee-bloom in the summer, and ruin their sheep-food in the spring.

"'True, quite true,' said Allo. 'How can we make our holy heather wine, if you burn our bee-pasture?'

"We talked long, Maximus asking keen questions that showed he knew much and had thought more about the Picts. He said presently to me: 'If I gave you the old Province of Valentia to govern, could you keep the Picts contented till I won Gaul? Stand away, so that you do not see Allo's face; and speak your own thoughts.'

"'No,' I said. 'You cannot remake that Province. The Picts have been free too long.'

"'Leave them their village councils, and let them furnish their own soldiers,' he said. 'You, I am sure, would hold the reins very lightly.'

"'Even then, no,' I said. 'At least not now. They have been too oppressed by us to trust anything with a Roman name for years and years.'

"I heard old Allo behind me mutter: 'Good child!'

"'Then what do you recommend,' said Maximus, 'to keep the North quiet till I win Gaul?'

"'Leave the Picts alone,' I said. 'Stop the heather-burning at once, and – they are improvident little animals – send them a shipload or two of corn now and then.'

"'Their own men must distribute it – not some cheating Greek accountant,' said Pertinax.

"'Yes, and allow them to come to our hospitals when they are sick,' I said.

"'Surely they would die first,' said Maximus.

"'Not if Parnesius brought them in,' said Allo. 'I could show you twenty wolf-bitten, bear-clawed Picts within twenty miles of here. But Parnesius must stay with them in hospital, else they would go mad with fear.'

"'*I* see,' said Maximus. 'Like everything else in the world, it is one man's work. You, I think, are that one man.'

"'Pertinax and I are one,' I said.

"'As you please, so long as you work. Now, Allo, you know that I mean your people no harm. Leave us to talk together,' said Maximus.

"'No need!' said Allo. 'I am the corn between the upper and lower millstones. I must know what the lower millstone means to do. These boys have spoken the truth as far as they know it. I, a Prince, will tell you the rest. I am troubled about the Men of the North.' He squatted like a hare in the heather, and looked over his shoulder.

"'I also,' said Maximus, 'or I should not be here.'

"'Listen,' said Allo. 'Long and long ago the Winged Hats' – he meant the Northmen – 'came to our beaches and said, "Rome falls! Push her down!" We fought you. You sent men. We were beaten. After that we said to the Winged Hats, "You are liars! Make our men alive that Rome killed, and we will believe you." They went away ashamed. Now they come back bold, and they tell the old tale, which we begin to believe – that Rome falls!'

"'Give me three years' peace on the Wall,' cried Maximus, 'and I will show you and all the ravens how they lie!'

"'Ah, I wish it too! I wish to save what is left of the corn from the millstones. But you shoot us Picts when we come to borrow a little iron from the Iron Ditch; you burn our heather, which is all our crop; you trouble us with your great catapults. Then you hide behind the Wall, and scorch us with Greek fire. How can I keep my young men from listening to the Winged Hats – in winter especially, when we are hungry? My young men will say, "Rome can neither fight nor rule. She is taking her men out of Britain. The Winged Hats will help us to push down the Wall. Let us show them the secret roads across the bogs." Do l want that? No!' He spat like an adder. 'I would keep the secrets of my people though I were burned alive. My two children here have spoken truth. Leave us Picts alone. Comfort us, and cherish us, and feed us from far off – with the hand behind the back. Parnesius understands us. Let *him* have rule on the Wall, and I will hold my young men quiet for' – he ticked it off on his fingers 'one year easily: the next year not so easily: the third year, perhaps! See, I give you three years. If then you do not show us that Rome is strong in men and terrible in arms, the Winged Hats, I tell you, will sweep down the Wall from either sea till they meet in the middle, and you will go. *I* shall not grieve over that, but well I know tribe never helps tribe except for one price. We Picts will go too. The Winged Hats will grind us to this!' He tossed a handful of dust in the air.

"'Oh, Roma Dea!' said Maximus, half aloud. 'It is always one man's work – always and everywhere!'

"'And one man's life,' said Allo. 'You are Emperor, but not a God. You may die.'

"'I have thought of that too,' said he. 'Very good. If this wind holds, I shall be at the East end of the Wall by morning. Tomorrow, then, I shall see you two when I inspect, and I will make you Captains of the Wall for this work.'

"'One instant, Caesar,' said Pertinax. 'All men have their price. I am not bought yet.'

"'Do *you* also begin to bargain so early?' said Maximus. 'Well?'

"'Give me justice against my uncle Icenus, the Duumvir of Divio in Gaul,' he said.

"'Only a life? I thought it would be money or an office. Certainly you shall have him. Write his name on these tablets – on the red side; the other is for the living!' and Maximus held out his tablets.

"'He is of no use to me dead,' said Pertinax. 'My mother is a widow. I am far off. I am not sure he pays her all her dowry.'

"'No matter. My arm is reasonably long. We will look through your uncle's accounts in due time. Now, farewell till tomorrow, O Captains of the Wall!'

"We saw him grow small across the heather as he walked to the galley. There were Picts, scores, each side of him, hidden behind stones. He never looked left or right. He sailed away southerly, full spread before the evening breeze, and when we had watched him out to sea, we were silent. We understood that Earth bred few men like to this man.

"Presently Allo brought the ponies and held them for us to mount – a thing he had never done before.

"'Wait awhile,' said Pertinax, and he made a little altar of cut turf, and strewed heather-bloom atop, and laid upon it a letter from a girl in Gaul.

"'What do you do, O my friend?' I said.

"'I sacrifice to my dead youth,' he answered, and, when the flames had consumed the letter, he ground them out with his heel. Then we rode back to that Wall of which we were to be Captains."

Parnesius stopped. The children sat still, not even asking if that were all the tale. Puck beckoned, and pointed the way out of the wood. "Sorry," he whispered, "but you must go now."

"We haven't made him angry, have we?" said Una. "He looks so far off, and – and – thinky."

"Bless your heart, no. Wait till tomorrow. It won't be long. Remember, you've been playing *Lays of Ancient Rome*."

And as soon as they had scrambled through their gap where Oak, Ash and Thorn grew, that was all they remembered.

A Song to Mithras

Mithras, God of the Morning, our trumpets waken the Wall!
"Rome is above the Nations, but Thou art over all!"
Now as the names are answered, and the guards are
     marched away,
Mithras, also a soldier, give us strength for the day!

Mithras, God of the Noontide, the heather swims in the heat,
Our helmets scorch our foreheads, our sandals burn our feet.
Now in the ungirt hour, now ere we blink and drowse,
Mithras, also a soldier, keep us true to our vows!

Mithras, God of the Sunset, low on the Western main,
Thou descending immortal, immortal to rise again!
Now when the watch is ended, now when the wine is drawn,
Mithras, also a soldier, keep us pure till the dawn!

Mithras, God of the Midnight, here where the great bull dies,
Look on Thy children in darkness. Oh, take our sacrifice!
Many roads Thou hast fashioned: all of them lead to the Light!
Mithras, also a soldier, teach us to die aright!

The Winged Hats

The next day happened to be what they called a Wild Afternoon. Father and Mother went out to pay calls; Miss Blake went for a ride on her bicycle, and they were left all alone till eight o'clock.

When they had seen their dear parents and their dear preceptress politely off the premises they got a cabbage-leaf full of raspberries from the gardener, and a Wild Tea from Ellen. They ate the raspberries to prevent their squashing, and they meant to divide the cabbage-leaf with Three Cows down at the Theatre, but they came across a dead hedgehog which they simply *had* to bury, and the leaf was too useful to waste.

Then they went on to the Forge and found old Hobden the hedger at home with his son, the Bee Boy, who is not quite right in his head, but who can pick up swarms of bees in his naked hands; and the Bee Boy told them the rhyme about the slow-worm:

> "If I had eyes *as* I could see,
> No mortal man would trouble me."

They all had tea together by the hives, and Hobden said the loaf-cake which Ellen had given them was almost as good as what his wife used to make, and he showed them how to set a wire at the right height for hares. They knew about rabbits already.

Then they climbed up Long Ditch into the lower end of Far Wood. This is sadder and darker than the Volaterrae end because of an old marl-pit full of black water, where weepy, hairy moss hangs round the stumps of the willows and alders. But the birds come to perch on the dead branches, and Hobden says that the bitter willow-water is a sort of medicine for sick animals.

They sat down on a felled oak-trunk in the shadows of the beech undergrowth, and were looping the wires Hobden had given them, when they saw Parnesius.

"How quietly you came!" said Una, moving up to make room. "Where's Puck?"

"The Faun and I have disputed whether it is better that I should tell you all my tale, or leave it untold," he replied.

"I only said that if he told it as it happened you wouldn't understand it," said Puck, jumping up like a squirrel from behind the log.

"I don't understand all of it," said Una, "but I like hearing about the little Picts."

"What *I* can't understand," said Dan, "is how Maximus knew all about the Picts when he was over in Gaul."

"He who makes himself Emperor anywhere must know everything, everywhere," said Parnesius. "We had this much from Maximus's mouth after the Games."

"Games? What Games?" said Dan.

Parnesius stretched his arm out stiffly, thumb pointed to the ground. "Gladiators! *That* sort of game," he said. "There were two days' Games in his honour when he landed all unexpected at Segedunum on the East end of the Wall. Yes, the day after we had met him we held two days' Games; but I think the greatest risk was run, not by the poor wretches on the sand, but by Maximus. In the old days the Legions kept silence before their Emperor. So did not we! You could hear the solid roar run West along the Wall as his chair was carried rocking through the crowds. The garrison beat round him – clamouring, clowning, asking for pay, for change of quarters, for anything that came into their wild heads. That chair was like a little boat among waves, dipping and falling, but always rising again after one had shut the eyes." Parnesius shivered.

"Were they angry with him?" said Dan.

"No more angry than wolves in a cage when their trainer walks among them. If he had turned his back an instant, or for an instant had ceased to hold their eyes, there would have been another Emperor made on the Wall that hour. Was it not so, Faun?"

"So it was. So it always will be," said Puck.

"Late in the evening his messenger came for us, and we followed to the Temple of Victory, where he lodged with Rutilianus, the General of the Wall. I had hardly seen the General before, but he always gave me leave when I wished to take Heather. He was a great glutton, and kept five Asian cooks, and he came of a family that believed in oracles. We could smell his good dinner when we entered, but the tables were empty. He lay snorting on a couch. Maximus sat apart among long rolls of accounts. Then the doors were shut."

"'These are your men,' said Maximus to the General, who propped his eye-corners open with his gouty fingers, and stared at us like a fish.

"'I shall know them again, Caesar,' said Rutilianus.

"'Very good,' said Maximus. 'Now hear! You are not to move man or shield on the Wall except as these boys shall tell you. You will do nothing, except eat, without their permission. They are the head and arms. You are the belly!'

"'As Caesar pleases,' the old man grunted. 'If my pay and profits are not cut, you may make my Ancestors' oracle my master. Rome has been! Rome has been!' Then he turned on his side to sleep.

"'He has it,' said Maximus. 'We will get to what *I* need.'

"He unrolled full copies of the number of men and supplies on the Wall – down to the sick that very day in Hunno Hospital. Oh, but I groaned when his pen marked off detachment after detachment of our best – of our least worthless men! He took two towers of our Scythians, two of our North British auxiliaries, two Numidian cohorts, the Dacians all, and half the Belgians. It was like an eagle pecking a carcass.

"'And now, how many catapults have you?' He turned up a new list, but Pertinax laid his open hand here.

"'No, Caesar,' said he. 'Do not tempt the Gods too far. Take me, or engines, but not both; else we refuse.'

"Engines?" said Una.

"The catapults of the Wall – huge things forty feet high to the head – firing nets of raw stone or forged bolts. Nothing can stand against them. He left us our catapults at last, but he took a Caesar's half of our men without pity. We were a shell when he rolled up the lists!

"'Hail, Caesar! We, about to die, salute you!' said Pertinax, laughing. 'If any enemy even leans against the Wall now, it will tumble.'

"'Give me the three years Allo spoke of,' he answered, 'and you shall have twenty thousand men of your own choosing up here. But now it is a gamble – a game played against the Gods, and the stakes are Britain, Gaul, and perhaps Rome. You play on my side?'

"'We will play, Caesar,' I said, for I had never met a man like this man.

"'Good. Tomorrow,' said he, 'I proclaim you Captains of the Wall before the troops.'

"So we went into the moonlight, where they were cleaning the ground after the Games. We saw great Roma Dea atop of the Wall, the frost on her helmet, and her spear pointed towards the North Star. We saw the twinkle of night -fires all along the guard-towers, and the line of the black catapults growing smaller and smaller in the distance. All these things we knew till we were weary; but that night they seemed very strange to us, because the next day we knew we were to be their masters.

"The men took the news well; but when Maximus went away with half our strength, and we had to spread ourselves into the emptied towers, and the townspeople complained that trade would be ruined, and the autumn gales blew – it was dark days for us two. Here Pertinax was more than my right hand. Being born and bred among the great country houses in Gaul, he knew the proper words to address to all – from Roman-born Centurions to those dogs of the Third – the Libyans. And he spoke to each as though that man were as high-minded as himself. Now *I* saw so strongly what things were needed to be done, that I forgot things are only accomplished by means of men. That was a mistake.

"I feared nothing from the Picts, at least for that year, but Allo warned me that the Winged Hats would soon come in from the sea at each end of the Wall to prove to the Picts how weak we were. So I made ready in haste, and none too soon. I shifted our best men to the ends of the Wall, and set up screened catapults by the beach. The Winged Hats would drive in before the snow-squalls ten or twenty boats at a time – on Segedunum or Ituna, according as the wind blew.

"Now a ship coming in to land men must furl her sail. If you wait till you see her men gather up the sail's foot, your catapults can jerk a net of loose stones (bolts only cut through the cloth) into the bag of it. Then she turns over, and the sea makes everything clean again. A few men may come ashore, but very few . . . It was not hard work, except the waiting on the beach in blowing sand and snow. And that was how we dealt with the Winged Hats that winter.

"Early in the spring, when the East winds blow like skinning-knives, they gathered again off Segedunum with many ships. Allo told me they would never rest till they had taken a tower in open fight. Certainly they fought in the open. We dealt with them thoroughly through a long day: and when all was finished, one man dived clear of the wreckage of his ship, and swam towards shore. I waited, and a wave tumbled him at my feet.

"As I stooped, I saw he wore such a medal as I wear." Parnesius raised his hand to his neck. "Therefore, when he could speak, I addressed him a certain Question which can only be answered in a certain manner. He answered with the necessary Word – the Word that belongs to the Degree of Gryphons in the science of Mithras my God. I put my shield over him till he could stand up. You see I am not short, but he was a head taller than I. He said: 'What now?' I said: 'At your pleasure, my brother, to stay or go.'

"He looked out across the surf. There remained one ship unhurt, beyond range of our catapults. I checked the catapults and he waved her in. She came as a hound comes to a master. When she was yet a hundred paces from the beach, he flung back his hair, and swam out. They hauled him in, and went away. I knew that those who worship Mithras are many and of all races, so I did not think much more upon the matter.

"A month later I saw Allo with his horses – by the Temple of Pan, O Faun – and he gave me a great necklace of gold studded with coral.

"At first I thought it was a bribe from some tradesman in the town – meant for old Rutilianus. 'Nay,' said Allo. 'This is a gift from Amal, that Winged Hat whom you saved on the beach. He says you are a Man.'

"'He is a Man, too. Tell him I can wear his gift,' I answered.

"'Oh, Amal is a young fool; but, speaking as sensible men, your Emperor is doing such great things in Gaul that the Winged Hats are anxious to be his friends, or, better still, the friends of his servants. They think you and Pertinax could lead them to victories.' Allo looked at me like a one-eyed raven.

"'Allo,' I said, 'you are the corn between the two millstones. Be content if they grind evenly, and don't thrust your hand between them."

"'I?' said Allo. 'I hate Rome and the Winged Hats equally; but if the Winged Hats thought that some day you and Pertinax might join them against Maximus, they would leave you in peace while you considered. Time is what we need – you and I and Maximus. Let me carry a pleasant message back to the Winged Hats – something for them to make a council over. We barbarians are all alike. We sit up half the night to discuss anything a Roman says. Eh?'

"'We have no men. We must fight with words,' said Pertinax. 'Leave it to Allo and me.'

"So Allo carried word back to the Winged Hats that we would not fight them if they did not fight us; and they (I think they were a little tired of losing men in the sea) agreed to a sort of truce. I believe Allo, who being a horse-dealer loved lies, also told them we might some day rise against Maximus as Maximus had risen against Rome."

"Indeed, they permitted the corn-ships which I sent to the Picts to pass North that season without harm. Therefore the Picts were well fed that winter, and since they were in some sort my children, I was glad of it. We had only two thousand men on the Wall, and I wrote many times to Maximus and begged – prayed – him to send me only one cohort of my old North British troops. He could not spare them. He needed them to win more victories in Gaul.

"Then came news that he had defeated and slain the Emperor Gratian, and thinking he must now be secure, I wrote again for men. He answered: *'You will learn that I have at last settled accounts with the pup Gratian. There was no need that he should have died, but he became confused and lost his head, which is a bad thing to befall any Emperor. Tell your Father I am content to drive two mules only; for unless my old General's son thinks himself destined to destroy me, I shall rest Emperor of Gaul and Britain, and then you, my two children, will presently get all the men you need. Just now I can spare none.'*

"What did he mean by his General's son?" said Dan.

"He meant Theodosius Emperor of Rome, who was the son of Theodosius the General under whom Maximus had fought in the old Pict War. The two men never loved each other, and when Gratian made the younger Theodosius Emperor of the East (at least, so I've heard), Maximus carried on the war to the second generation. It was his fate, and it was his fall. But Theodosius the Emperor is a good man. As I know." Parnesius was silent for a moment and then continued.

"I wrote back to Maximus that, though we had peace on the Wall, I should be happier with a few more men and some new catapults. He answered: *'You must live a little longer under the shadow of my victories, till I can see what young Theodosius intends. He may welcome me as a brother Emperor, or he may be preparing an army. In either case I cannot spare men just now.'*

"But he was always saying that," cried Una.

"It was true. He did not make excuses; but thanks, as he said, to the news of his victories, we had no trouble on the Wall for a long, long time. The Picts grew fat as their own sheep among the heather, and as many of my men as lived were well exercised in their weapons. Yes, the Wall looked strong. For myself, I knew how weak we were. I knew that if even a false rumour of any defeat to Maximus broke loose among the Winged Hats, they might come down in earnest, and then – the Wall must go! For the Picts I never cared, but in those years I learned something of the strength of the Winged Hats. They increased their strength every day, but I could not increase my men. Maximus had emptied Britain behind us, and I felt myself to be a man with a rotten stick standing before a broken fence to turn bulls.

"Thus, my friends, we lived on the Wall, waiting, waiting – waiting for the men that Maximus never sent.

"Presently he wrote that he was preparing an army against Theodosius. He wrote – and Pertinax read it over my shoulder in our quarters: '*Tell your Father that my destiny orders me to drive three mules or be torn in pieces by them. I hope within a year to finish with Theodosius, son of Theodosius, once and for all. Then you shall have Britain to rule, and Pertinax, if he chooses, Gaul. Today I wish strongly you were with me to beat my Auxiliaries into shape. Do not, I pray you, believe any rumour of my sickness. I have a little evil in my old body which I shall cure by riding swiftly into Rome.*'

"Said Pertinax: 'It is finished with Maximus. He writes as a man without hope. I, a man without hope, can see this. What does he add at the bottom of the roll? *"Tell Pertinax I have met his late Uncle, the Duumvir of Divio, and that he accounted to me quite truthfully for all his Mother's monies. I have sent her with a fitting escort, for she is the mother of a hero, to Nicaea, where the climate is warm."*'

"'That is proof,' said Pertinax. 'Nicaea is not far by sea from Rome. A woman there could take ship and fly to Rome in time of war. Yes, Maximus foresees his death, and is fulfilling his promises one by one. But I am glad my uncle met him.'

"'You think blackly today?' I asked.

"'I think truth. The Gods weary of the play we have played against them. Theodosius will destroy Maximus. It is finished!'

"'Will you write him that?' I said.

"'See what I shall write,' he answered, and he took pen and wrote a letter cheerful as the light of day, tender as a woman's and full of jests. Even I, reading over his shoulder, took comfort from it till – I saw his face!'

"'And now,' he said, sealing it, 'we be two dead men, my brother. Let us go to the Temple.'

"We prayed awhile to Mithras, where we had many times

prayed before. After that, we lived day by day among evil rumours till winter came again.''

"It happened one morning that we rode to the East shore, and found on the beach a fair-haired man, half frozen, bound to some broken planks. Turning him over, we saw by his belt-buckle that he was a Goth of an Eastern Legion. Suddenly he opened his eyes and cried loudly, 'He is dead! The letters were with me, but the Winged Hats sank the ship.' So saying, he died between our hands.

"We asked not who was dead. We knew! We raced before the driving snow to Hunno, thinking perhaps Allo might be there. We found him already at our stables, and he saw by our faces what we had heard.

"'It was in a tent by the sea,' he stammered. 'He was be-headed by Theodosius. He sent a letter to you, written while he waited to be slain. The Winged Hats met the ship and took it. The news is running through the heather like fire. Blame me not! I cannot hold back my young men any more.'

"'I would we could say as much for our men,' said Pertinax, laughing. 'But, Gods be praised, they cannot run away.'

"'What do you do?' said Allo. 'I bring an order – a mes-sage – from the Winged Hats that you join them with your men, and march South to plunder Britain.'

"'It grieves me,' said Pertinax, 'but we are stationed here to stop that thing.'

"'If I carry back such an answer they will kill me,' said Allo. 'I always promised the Winged Hats that you would rise when Maximus fell. I – I did not think he could fall.'

"'Alas! my poor barbarian,' said Pertinax, still laughing. 'Well, you have sold us too many good ponies to be thrown back to your friends. We will make you a prisoner, although you are an ambassador.'

"'Yes, that will be best,' said Allo, holding out a halter. We bound him lightly, for he was an old man.

"'Presently the Winged Hats may come to look for you, and that will give us more time. See how the habit of playing for time sticks to a man!' said Pertinax, as he tied the rope.

"'No,' I said. 'Time may help. If Maximus wrote us a letter while he was a prisoner, Theodosius must have sent the ship that brought it. If he can send ships, he can send men.'

"'How will that profit us?' said Pertinax. 'We serve Maximus, not Theodosius. Even if by some miracle of the Gods Theodosius down South sent and saved the Wall, we could not expect more than the death Maximus died.'

"'It concerns us to defend the Wall, no matter what Emperor dies, or makes die,' I said.

"'That is worthy of your brother the philosopher,' said Pertinax. 'Myself I am without hope, so I do not say solemn and stupid things! Rouse the Wall!'

"We armed the Wall from end to end; we told the officers that there was a rumour of Maximus's death which might bring down the Winged Hats, but we were sure, even if it were true, that Theodosius, for the sake of Britain, would send us help. Therefore, we must stand fast . . . My friends, it is above all things strange to see how men bear ill news! Often the strongest till then become the weakest, while the weakest, as it were, reach up and steal strength from the Gods. So it was with us. Yet my Pertinax by his jests and his courtesy and his labours had put heart and training into our poor numbers during the past years – more than I should have thought possible. Even our Libyan Cohort – the Third – stood up in their padded cuirasses and did not whimper.

"In three days came seven chiefs and elders of the Winged Hats. Among them was that tall young man, Amal, whom I had met on the beach, and he smiled when he saw my necklace. We made them welcome, for they were ambassadors. We showed them Allo, alive but bound. They thought we had killed him, and I saw it would not have vexed them if we had. Allo saw it too, and it vexed him. Then in our quarters at Hunno we came to council.

"They said that Rome was falling, and that we must join them. They offered me all South Britain to govern after they had taken a tribute out of it.

"I answered, 'Patience. This Wall is not weighed off like plunder. Give me proof that my General is dead.'

"'Nay,' said one elder, 'prove to us that he lives'; and another said cunningly, 'What will you give us if we read you his last words?'

"'We are not merchants to bargain,' cried Amal. 'Moreover, I owe this man my life. He shall have his proof.' He threw across to me a letter (well I knew the seal) from Maximus.

"'We took this out of the ship we sank,' he cried. 'I cannot read, but I know one sign, at least, which makes me believe.' He showed me a dark stain on the outer roll that my heavy heart perceived was the valiant blood of Maximus.

"'Read!' said Amal. 'Read, and then let us hear whose servants you are!'

"Said Pertinax, very softly, after he had looked through it: 'I will read it all. Listen, barbarians!' He read that which I have carried next my heart ever since."

Parnesius drew from his neck a folded and spotted piece of parchment, and began in a hushed voice:

"*To Parnesius and Pertinax, the not unworthy Captains of the Wall, from Maximus, once Emperor of Gaul and Britain, now prisoner waiting death by the sea in the camp of Theodosius – Greeting and Goodbye!*"

"'Enough,' said young Amal; 'there is your proof! You must join us now!'

"Pertinax looked long and silently at him, till that fair man blushed like a girl. Then read Pertinax:

'*I have joyfully done much evil in my life to those who*

*have wished me evil, but if ever I did any evil to you two I
repent, and I ask your forgiveness. The three mules which I
strove to drive have torn me in pieces as your Father
prophesied. The naked swords wait at the tent door to give
me the death I gave to Gratian. Therefore I, your General
and your Emperor, send you free and honourable dismissal
from my service, which you entered, not for money or office,
but, as it makes me warm to believe, because you loved
me!'"*

"'By the Light of the Sun,' Amal broke in. 'This was in
some sort a Man! We may have been mistaken in his
servants!'

"And Pertinax read on: *'You gave me the time for which I
asked. If I have failed to use it, do not lament. We have
gambled very splendidly against the Gods, but they hold
weighted dice, and I must pay the forfeit. Remember, I have
been; but Rome is; and Rome will be. Tell Pertinax his
Mother is in safety at Nicaea, and her monies are in charge
of the Prefect at Antipolis. Make my remembrances to your
Father and to your Mother, whose friendship was great
gain to me. Give also to my little Picts and to the Winged
Hats such messages as their thick heads can understand. I
would have sent you three Legions this very day if all had
gone aright. Do not forget me. We have worked together.
Farewell! Farewell! Farewell!'*

"Now, that was my Emperor's last letter." (The children
heard the parchment crackle as Parnesius returned it to its
place.)

"'I was mistaken,' said Amal. 'The servants of such a
man will sell nothing except over the sword. I am glad of
it.' He held out his hand to me.

"'But Maximus has given you your dismissal,' said an
elder. 'You are certainly free to serve – or to rule – whom
you please. Join – do not follow – join us!'

"'We thank you,' said Pertinax. 'But Maximus tells us to

give you such messages as – pardon me, but I use his words – your thick heads can understand.' He pointed through the door to the foot of a catapult wound up.

"'We understand,' said an elder. 'The Wall must be won at a price?'

"'It grieves me,' said Pertinax, laughing, 'but so it must be won,' and he gave them of our best Southern wine.

"They drank, and wiped their yellow beards in silence till they rose to go.

"Said Amal, stretching himself (for they were barbarians) 'We be a goodly company; I wonder what the ravens and the dogfish will make of some of us before this snow melts.'

"'Think rather what Theodosius may send,' I answered; and though they laughed, I saw that my chance shot troubled them.

"Only old Allo lingered behind a little.

"'You see,' he said, winking and blinking, 'I am no more than their dog. When I have shown their men the secret short ways across our bogs, they will kick me like one.'

"'Then I should not be in haste to show them those ways,' said Pertinax, 'till I was sure that Rome could not save the Wall.'

"'You think so? Woe is me!' said the old man. 'I only wanted peace for my people,' and he went out stumbling through the snow behind the tall Winged Hats.

"In this fashion then, slowly, a day at a time, which is very bad for doubting troops, the War came upon us. At first the Winged Hats swept in from the sea as they had done before, and there we met them as before – with the catapults; and they sickened of it. Yet for a long time they would not trust their duck-legs on land, and I think, when it came to revealing the secrets of the tribe, the little Picts were afraid or ashamed to show them all the roads across the heather. I had this from a Pict prisoner. They were as much our spies as our enemies, for the Winged Hats oppressed them, and took their winter stores. Ah, foolish Little People!

"Then the Winged Hats began to roll us up from each end of the Wall. I sent runners Southward to see what the news might be in Britain, but the wolves were very bold that winter, among the deserted stations where the troops had once been, and none came back. We had trouble, too, with the forage for the ponies along the Wall. I kept ten, and so did Pertinax. We lived and slept in the saddle, riding east or west, and we ate our worn-out ponies. The people of the town also made us some trouble till I gathered them all in one quarter behind Hunno. We broke down the Wall on either side of it to make as it were a citadel. Our men fought better in close order.

"By the end of the second month we were deep in the War as a man is deep in a snowdrift, or in a dream. I think we fought in our sleep. At least I know I have gone on the Wall and come off again, remembering nothing between, though my throat was harsh with giving orders, and my sword, I could see, had been used.

"The Winged Hats fought like wolves – all in a pack. Where they had suffered most, there they charged in most hotly. This was hard for the defenders, but it held them from sweeping on into Britain.

"In those days Pertinax and I wrote on the plaster of the bricked archway into Valentia the names of the towers, and the days on which they fell one by one. We wished for some record.

"And the fighting? The fight was always hottest to left and right of the great statue of Roma Dea, near to Rutilianus's house. By the Light of the Sun, that old fat man, whom we had not considered at all, grew young again among the trumpets! I remember he said his sword was an oracle! 'Let us consult the Oracle,' he would say, and put the handle against his ear, and shake his head wisely. 'And *this* day is allowed Rutilianus to live,' he would say, and, tucking up his cloak, he would puff and pant and fight well. Oh, there were jests in plenty on the Wall to take the place of food!

"We endured for two months and seventeen days always being pressed from three sides into a smaller space. Several times Allo sent in word that help was at hand. We did not believe it, but it cheered our men.

"The end came not with shoutings of joy, but, like the rest, as in a dream. The Winged Hats suddenly left us in peace for one night and the next day; which is too long for spent men. We slept at first lightly, expecting to be roused, and then like logs, each where he lay. May you never need such sleep! When I waked our towers were full of strange, armed men, who watched us snoring. I roused Pertinax, and we leaped up together.

"'What?' said a young man in clean armour. 'Do you fight against Theodosius? Look!'

"North we looked over the red snow. No Winged Hats were there. South we looked over the white snow, and behold there were the Eagles of two strong Legions encamped. East and west we saw flame and fighting, but by Hunno all was still.

"'Trouble no more,' said the young man. 'Rome's arm is long. Where are the Captains of the Wall?'

"We said we were those men.

"'But you are old and grey-haired,' he cried. 'Maximus said that they were boys.'

"'Yes, that was true some years ago,' said Pertinax. 'What is our fate to be, you fine and well-fed child?'

"'I am called Ambrosius, a secretary of the Emperor,' he answered. 'Show me a certain letter which Maximus wrote from a tent at Aquileia, and perhaps I will believe.'

"I took it from my breast, and when he had read it he saluted us, saying: 'Your fate is in your own hands. If you choose to serve Theodosius, he will give you a Legion. If it suits you to go to your homes, we will give you a Triumph.'

"'I would like better a bath, wine, food, razors, soaps, oils, and scents,' said Pertinax, laughing.

"'Oh, I see you are a boy,' said Ambrosius. 'And you?' turning to me.

"'We bear no ill-will against Theodosius, but in War – ' I began.

"'In War it is as it is in Love,' said Pertinax. 'Whether she be good or bad, one gives one's best once, to one only. That given, there remains no second worth giving or taking.'

"'That is true,' said Ambrosius. 'I was with Maximus before he died. He warned Theodosius that you would never serve him, and frankly I say I am sorry for my Emperor.'

"'He has Rome to console him,' said Pertinax. 'I ask you of your kindness to let us go to our homes and get this smell out of our nostrils.'

"None the less they gave us a Triumph!"

"It was well earned," said Puck, throwing some leaves into the still water of the marlpit. The black, oily circles spread dizzily as the children watched them.

"I want to know, oh, ever so many things," said Dan. "What happened to old Allo? Did the Winged Hats ever come back? And what did Amal do?"

"And what happened to the fat old General with the five cooks?" said Una. "And what did your Mother say when you came home?"

"She'd say you're settin' too long over this old pit, so late as 'tis already," said old Hobden's voice behind them. "Hst!" he whispered.

He stood still, for not twenty paces away a magnificent dog-fox sat on his haunches and looked at the children as though he were an old friend of theirs.

"Oh, Mus' Reynolds, Mus' Reynolds!" said Hobden, under his breath. "If I knowed all was inside your head, I'd know something wuth knowin'. Mus' Dan an' Miss Una, come along o' me while I lock up my liddle hen-house."

A Pict Song

Rome never looks where she treads,
　　Always her heavy hooves fall
On our stomachs, our hearts or our heads;
　　And Rome never heeds when we bawl.
Her sentries pass on – that is all,
　　And we gather behind them in hordes,
And plot to reconquer the Wall,
　　With only our tongues for our swords.

We are the Little Folk – we!
　　Too little to love or to hate.
Leave us alone and you'll see
　　How we can drag down the Great!
We are the worm in the wood!
　　We are the rot in the root!
We are the germ in the blood!
　　We are the thorn in the foot!

Mistletoe killing an oak –
　　Rats gnawing cables in two –
Moths making holes in a cloak –
　　How they must love what they do!
Yes – and we Little Folk too,
　　We are as busy as they –
Working our works out of view –
　　Watch, and you'll see it some day!

No indeed! We are not strong,
  But we know Peoples that are.
Yes, and we'll guide them along,
  To smash and destroy you in War!
We shall be slaves just the same?
  Yes, we have always been slaves,
But you – you will die of the shame,
  And then we shall dance on your graves!

We are the Little Folk, we, etc.

Hal o' the Draft

Prophets have honour all over the Earth,
    Except in the village where they were born,
Where such as knew them boys from birth
    Nature-ally hold 'em in scorn.

When Prophets are naughty and young and vain,
    They make a won'erful grievance of it;
(You can see by their writings how they complain),
    But Oh, 'tis won'erful good for the Prophet!

There's nothing Nineveh Town can give
    (Nor being swallowed by whales between),
Makes up for the place where a man's folk live,
    That don't care nothing what he has been.
He might ha' been that, or he might ha' been this,
    But they love and they hate him for what he is.

A rainy afternoon drove Dan and Una over to play pirates in the Little Mill. If you don't mind rats on the rafters and oats in your shoes, the mill-attic, with its trap-doors and inscriptions on beams about floods and sweethearts, is a splendid place. It is lighted by a foot-square window, called Duck Window, that looks across to Little Lindens Farm, and the spot where Jack Cade was killed.

When they had climbed the attic ladder (they called it "the mainmast tree", out of the ballad of Sir Andrew Barton, and Dan "swarved it with might and main", as the ballad says) they saw a man sitting on Duck Window-sill. He was dressed in a plum-coloured doublet and tight

144

plum-coloured hose, and he drew busily in a red-edged
book.

"Sit ye! Sit ye!" Puck cried from a rafter overhead. "See
what it is to be beautiful! Sir Harry Dawe – pardon, Hal –
says I am the very image of a head for a gargoyle."

The man laughed and raised his dark velvet cap to the
children, and his grizzled hair bristled out in a stormy
fringe. He was old – forty at least – but his eyes were
young, with funny little wrinkles all round them. A satchel
of embroidered leather hung from his broad belt, which
looked interesting.

"May we see?" said Una, coming forward.

"Surely – sure-ly!" he said, moving up on the window-
seat, and returned to his work with a silver-pointed pencil.
Puck sat as though the grin were fixed for ever on his broad
face, while they watched the quick, certain fingers that cop-
ied it. Presently the man took a reed pen from his satchel,
and trimmed it with a little ivory knife, carved in the sem-
blance of a fish.

"Oh, what a beauty!" cried Dan.

"'Ware fingers! That blade is perilous sharp. I made it
myself of the best Low Country crossbow steel. And so,
too, this fish. When his back-fin travels to his tail – so – it
swallows up the blade, even as the whale swallowed Gaffer
Jonah . . . Yes, and that's my inkhorn. I made the four silver
saints round it. Press Barnabas's head. It opens, and then –"
He dipped the trimmed pen, and with careful boldness began to put in the essential lines of Puck's rugged face, that
had been but faintly revealed by the silver point.

The children gasped, for it fairly leaped from the page.

As he worked, and the rain fell on the tiles, he talked –
now clearly, now muttering, now breaking off to frown or
smile at his work. He told them he was born at Little
Lindens Farm, and his father used to beat him for drawing
things instead of doing things, till an old priest called Fa-

ther Roger, who drew illuminated letters in rich people's books, coaxed the parents to let him take the boy as a sort of painter's apprentice. Then he went with Father Roger to Oxford, where he cleaned plates and carried cloaks and shoes for the scholars of a College called Merton.

"Didn't you hate that?" said Dan after a great many other questions.

"I never thought on't. Half Oxford was building new colleges or beautifying the old, and she had called to her aid the master-craftsmen of all Christendie – kings in their trade and honoured of Kings. I knew them. I worked for them: that was enough. No wonder – " He stopped and laughed.

"You became a great man, Hal," said Puck.

"They said so, Robin. Even Bramante said so."

"Why? What did you do?" Dan asked.

The artist looked at him queerly. "Things in stone and such, up and down England. You would not have heard of 'em. To come nearer home, I rebuilded this little St Barnabas' church of ours. It cost me more trouble and sorrow than aught I've touched in my life. But 'twas a sound lesson."

"Um," said Dan. "We've had lessons this morning."

"I'll not afflict ye, lad," said Hal, while Puck roared. "Only 'tis strange to think how that little church was re-built, re-roofed, and made glorious, thanks to some few godly Sussex ironmasters, a Bristow sailor lad, a proud ass called Hal o' the Draft because, d'you see, he was always drawing and drafting; and" – he dragged the words slowly – "*and* a Scotch pirate."

"Pirate?" said Dan. He wriggled like a hooked fish.

"Even that Andrew Barton you were singing of on the stair just now." He dipped again in the inkwell, and held his breath over a sweeping line, as though he had forgotten everything else.

"Pirates don't build churches, do they?" said Dan. "Or *do* they?"

"They help mightily," Hal laughed. "But you were at your lessons this morn, Jack Scholar."

"Oh, pirates aren't lessons. It was only Bruce and his silly old spider," said Una. "Why did Sir Andrew Barton help you?"

"I question if he ever knew it," said Hal, twinkling. "Robin, how a' mischief's name am I to tell these innocents what comes of sinful pride?"

"Oh, we know all about *that*," said Una pertly. "If you get too beany – that's cheeky – you get sat upon, of course."

Hal considered a moment, pen in air, and Puck said some long words.

"Aha! that was my case too," he cried. "Beany – you say – but certainly I did not conduct myself well. I was proud of – of such things as porches – a Galilee porch at Lincoln for choice – proud of one Torrigiano's arm on my shoulder, proud of my knighthood when I made the gilt scroll-work for the *Sovereign* – our King's ship. But Father Roger sitting in Merton College Library, he did not forget me. At the top of my pride, when I and no other should have builded the porch at Lincoln, he laid it on me with a terrible forefinger to go back to my Sussex clays and rebuild, at my own charges, my own church, where us Dawes have been buried for six generations. 'Out! Son of my Art!' said he. 'Fight the Devil at home ere you call yourself a man and a craftsman.' And I quaked, and I went . . . How's yon, Robin?" He flourished the finished sketch before Puck.

"Me! Me past peradventure," said Puck, smirking like a man at a mirror. "Ah, see! The rain has took off! I hate housen in daylight."

"Whoop! Holiday!" cried Hal, leaping up. "Who's for my Little Lindens? We can talk there."

They tumbled downstairs, and turned past the dripping willows by the sunny mill dam.

"Body o' me," said Hal, staring at the hop-garden, where

the hops were just ready to blossom. "What are these? Vines? No, not vines, and they twine the wrong way to beans." He began to draw in his ready book.

"Hops. New since your day," said Puck. "They're an herb of Mars, and their flowers dried flavour ale. We say –

> "Turkeys, Heresy, Hops, and Beer
> Came into England all in one year."

"Heresy I know. I've seen Hops – God be praised for their beauty! What is your Turkis?"

The children laughed. They knew the Lindens turkeys, and as soon as they reached Lindens orchard on the hill the full flock charged at them.

Out came Hal's book at once. "Hoity-toity!" he cried "Here's Pride in purple feathers! Here's wrathy contempt and the Pomps of the Flesh! How d'you call *them?*"

"Turkeys! Turkeys!" the children shouted, as the old gobbler raved and flamed against Hal's plum-coloured hose.

"'Save Your Magnificence!" he said. "I've drafted two good new things today." And he doffed his cap to the bubbling bird.

Then they walked through the grass to the knoll where Little Lindens stands. The old farmhouse, weather-tiled to the ground, took almost the colour of a blood-ruby in the afternoon light. The pigeons pecked at the mortar in the chimney-stacks; the bees that had lived under the tiles since it was built filled the hot August air with their booming; and the smell of the box-tree by the dairy-window mixed with the smell of earth after rain, bread after baking, and a tickle of wood-smoke.

The farmer's wife came to the door, baby on arm, shaded her brows against the sun, stooped to pluck a sprig of rosemary, and turned down the orchard. The old spaniel in his barrel barked once or twice to show he was in charge of the empty house. Puck clicked back the garden gate.

"D'you marvel that I love it?" said Hal, in a whisper "What can town folk know of the nature of housen – or land?"

They perched themselves arow on the old hacked oak bench in Lindens garden, looking across the valley of the brook at the fern-covered dimples and hollows of the Forge behind Hobden's cottage. The old man was cutting a faggot in his garden by the hives. It was quite a second after his chopper fell that the chump of the blow reached their lazy ears.

"Eh – yeh!" said Hal. "I mind when where that old gaffer stands was Nether Forge – Master John Collins's foundry. Many a night has his big trip-hammer shook me in my bed here. *Boom-bitty! Boom-bitty!* If the wind was east, I could hear Master Tom Collins's forge at Stockens answering his brother, *Boom-oop! Boom-oop!* and midway between, Sir John Pelham's sledgehammers at Brightling would strike in like a pack o' scholars, and '*Hic-haec-hoc*' they'd say, '*Hic-haec-hoc*,' till I fell asleep. Yes. The valley was as full o' forges and fineries as a May shaw o' cuckoos. All gone to grass now!"

"What did they make?" said Dan.

"Guns for the King's ships – and for others. Serpentines and cannon mostly. When the guns were cast, down would come the King's Officers, and take our plough-oxen to haul them to the coast. Look! Here's one of the first and finest craftsmen of the Sea!"

He fluttered back a page of his book, and showed them a young man's head. Underneath was written: "Sebastianus."

"He came down with a King's Order on Master John Collins for twenty serpentines (wicked little cannon they be!) to furnish a venture of ships. I drafted him thus sitting by our fire telling Mother of the new lands he'd find the far side the world. And he found them, too! There's a nose to cleave through unknown seas! Cabot was his name – a

Bristol lad – half a foreigner. I set a heap by him. He helped me to my church-building."

"I thought that was Sir Andrew Barton," said Dan.

"Ay, but foundations before roofs," Hal answered.

"Sebastian first put me in the way of it. I had come down here, not to serve God as a craftsman should, but to show my people how great a craftsman I was. They cared not, and it served me right, one split straw for my craft or my greatness. What a murrain call had I, they said, to mell with old St Barnabas'? Ruinous the church had been since the Black Death, and ruinous she would remain; and I could hang myself in my new scaffold-ropes! Gentle and simple, high and low – the Hayes, the Fowles, the Fenners, the Collinses – they were all in a tale against me. Only Sir John Pelham up yonder at Brightling bade me heart-up and go on. Yet how could I? Did I ask Master Collins for his timber tug to haul beams? The oxen had gone to Lewes after lime. Did he promise me a set of iron cramps or ties for the roof? They never came to hand, or else they were spaulty or cracked. So with everything. Nothing said, but naught done except I stood by them, and then done amiss. I thought the countryside was fair bewitched."

"It was, sure-ly," said Puck, knees under chin. "Did you never suspect anyone?"

"Not till Sebastian came for his guns, and John Collins played him the same dog's tricks as he'd played me with my ironwork. Week in, week out, two of three serpentines would be flawed in the casting, and only fit, they said, to be re-melted. Then John Collins would shake his head, and vow he could pass no cannon for the King's service that were not perfect. Saints! How Sebastian stormed! *I* know, for we sat on this bench sharing our sorrows inter-common.

"When Sebastian had fumed away six weeks at Lindens and gotten just six serpentines, Dirk Brenzett, Master of the *Cygnet* hoy, sends me word that the block of stone he was fetching me from France for our new font he'd hove overboard to lighten his ship, chased by Andrew Barton up to Rye Port."

"Ah! The pirate!" said Dan.

"Yes. And while I am tearing my hair over this, Ticehurst Will, my best mason, comes to me shaking, and vowing that the Devil, homed, tailed, and chained, has run out on him from the church-tower, and the men would work there no more. So I took 'em off the foundations, which we were strengthening, and went into the Bell Tavern for a cup of ale. Says Master John Collins: 'Have it your own way, lad; but if I was you, I'd take the sinnification o' the sign, and leave old Barnabas' Church alone!' And they all wagged their sinful heads, and agreed. Less afraid of the Devil than of me – as I saw later.

"When I brought my sweet news to Lindens, Sebastian was limewashing the kitchen-beams for Mother. He loved her like a son.

"'Cheer up, lad,' he says. 'God's where He was. Only you and I chance to be pure pute asses. We've been tricked, Hal, and more shame to me, a sailor, that I did not guess it before! You must leave your belfry alone, forsooth, because the Devil is adrift there; and I cannot get my serpentines because John Collins cannot cast them aright. Meantime Andrew Barton hawks off the Port of Rye. And why? To take those very serpentines which poor Cabot must whistle for; the said serpentines, I'll wager my share of new continents, being now hid away in St Barnabas' church tower. Clear as the Irish coast at noonday!'

"'They'd sure never dare to do it,' I said; 'and, for another thing, selling cannon to the King's enemies is black treason – hanging and fine.'

"'It is sure, large profit. Men'll dare any gallows for that. I have been a trader myself," says he. "We must be upsides with 'em for the honour of Bristol."

"Then he hatched a plot, sitting on the limewash bucket. We gave out to ride o' Tuesday to London and made a show of taking farewells of our friends – especially of Master John Collins. But at Wadhurst Woods we turned; rode home to the water-meadows; hid our horses in a willow-tot at the foot of the glebe, and, come night, stole a-tiptoe uphill to Barnabas' church again. A thick mist, and a moon striking through.

"I had no sooner locked the tower door behind us than over goes Sebastian full length in the dark.

"'Pest!' he says. 'Step high and feel low, Hal. I've stumbled over guns before.'

"I groped, and one by one – the tower was pitchy dark I counted the lither barrels of twenty serpentines laid out on pease straw. No conceal at all!

"'There's two demi-cannon my end,' says Sebastian, slapping metal. 'They'll be for Andrew Barton's lower deck. Honest – honest John Collins! So this is his warehouse, his arsenal, his armoury! Now see you why your pokings and pryings have raised the Devil in Sussex? You've hindered John's lawful trade for months,' and he laughed where he lay.

"A clay-cold tower is no fireside at midnight, so we climbed the belfry stairs, and there Sebastian trips over a cow-hide with its horns and tail.

"Aha! Your Devil has left his doublet! Does it become me, Hal?" He draws it on and capers in the slits of window-moonlight – won'erful devilish-like. Then he sits on the stairs, rapping with his tail on a board, and his back-aspect was dreader than his front, and a howlet lit in, and screeched at the horns of him.

"'If you'd keep out the Devil, shut the door,' he whispered. 'And that's another false proverb, Hal, for I can hear your tower door opening.'

"'I locked it. Who a-plague has another key, then?' I said.

"'All the congregation, to judge by their feet,' he says,

and peers into the blackness. 'Still! Still, Hal! Hear 'em grunt! That's more o' my serpentines, I'll be bound. One – two – three – four they bear in! Faith, Andrew equips himself like an Admiral! Twenty-four serpentines in all!'

"As if it had been an echo, we heard John Collins's voice come up all hollow: 'Twenty-four serpentines and two demi-cannon. That's the full tally for Sir Andrew Barton.'

"'Courtesy costs naught,' whispers Sebastian. 'Shall I drop my dagger on his head?'

"'They go over to Rye o' Thursday in the wool-wains, hid under the wool-packs. Dirk Brenzett meets them at Udimore, as before,' says John.

"'Lord! What a worn, handsmooth trade it is!' says Sebastian. 'I lay we are the sole two babes in the village that have not our lawful share in the venture.'

"There was a full score folk below, talking like all Robertsbridge Market. We counted them by voice.

"Master John Collins pipes: 'The guns for the French carrack must lie here next month. Will, when does your young fool' (me, so please you!) 'come back from Lunnon?'

"'No odds,' I heard Ticehurst Will answer. 'Lay 'em just where you've a mind, Mus' Collins. We're all too afraid o' the Devil to mell with the tower now.' And the long knave laughed.

"'Ah! 'tis easy enow for you to raise the Devil, Will,' says another – Ralph Hobden of the Forge.

"'Aaa-men!' roars Sebastian, and ere I could hold him, he leaps down the stairs – won'erful devilish-like – howling no bounds. He had scarce time to lay out for the nearest than they ran. Saints, how they ran! We heard them pound on the door of the Bell Tavern, and then we ran too.

"'What's next?' says Sebastian, looping up his cowtail as he leaped the briars. 'I've broke honest John's face.'

"'Ride to Sir John Pelham's,' I said. 'He is the only one that ever stood by me.'"

"We rode to Brightling, and past Sir John's lodges, where the keepers would have shot at us for deer-stealers, and we had Sir John down into his Justice's chair, and when we had told him our tale and showed him the cowhide which Sebastian wore still girt about him, he laughed till the tears ran.

"'Wel-a-well!' he says. 'I'll see justice done before daylight. What's your complaint? Master Collins is my old friend.'

"'He's none of mine,' I cried. 'When I think how he and his likes have baulked and dozened and cozened me at every turn over the church' – and I choked at the thought.

"'Ah, but ye see now they needed it for another use,' says he smoothly.

"'So they did my serpentines,' Sebastian cries. 'I should be half across the Western Ocean by now if my guns had been ready. But they're sold to a Scotch pirate by your old friend.'

"'Where's your proof?' says Sir John, stroking his beard.

"'I broke my shins over them not an hour since, and I heard John give order where they were to be taken,' says Sebastian.

"'Words! Words only,' says SirJohn. 'Master Collins is somewhat of a liar at best.'

"He carried it so gravely that, for the moment, I thought he was dipped in this secret traffick too, and that there was not an honest ironmaster in Sussex.

"'Name o' Reason!' says Sebastian, and raps with his cow-tail on the table, 'whose guns are they, then?'

"'Yours, manifestly,' says Sir John. 'You come with the King's Order for 'em, and Master Collins casts them in his foundry. If he chooses to bring them up from Nether Forge and lay 'em out in the church-tower, why they are e'en so much the nearer to the main road and you are saved a day's hauling. What a coil to make of a mere act of neighbourly kindness, lad!'

"'I fear I have requited him very scurvily,' says Sebastian, looking at his knuckles. 'But what of the demi-cannon? I could do with 'em well, but they are not in the King's Order.'

"'Kindness – loving kindness,' says Sir John. 'Questionless, in his zeal for the King and his love for you, John adds those two cannon as a gift. 'Tis plain as this coming daylight, ye stockfish!'

"'So it is,' says Sebastian. 'Oh, SirJohn, SirJohn, why did you never use the sea? You are lost ashore.' And he looked on him with great love.

"'I do my best in my station.' Sir John strokes his beard again and rolls forth his deep drumming Justice's voice thus: 'But – suffer me! – you two lads, on some midnight frolic into which I probe not, roystering around the taverns, surprise Master Collins at his' – he thinks a moment – 'at his good deeds done by stealth. Ye surprise him, I say, cruelly.'

"'Truth, Sir John. If you had seen him run!' says Sebastian.

"'On this you ride breakneck to me with a tale of pirates, and wool-wains, and cowhides, which, though it hath moved my mirth as a man, offendeth my reason as a magistrate. So I will e'en accompany you back to the tower with, perhaps, some few of my own people, and three-four wagons, and I'll be your warrant that Master John Collins will freely give you your guns and your demi-cannon, Master Sebastian.' He breaks into his proper voice – 'I warned the old tod and his neighbours long ago that they'd come to trouble with their side-sellings and bye-dealings; but we cannot have half Sussex hanged for a little gun-running. Are ye content lads?'

"'I'd commit any treason for two demi-cannon,' said Sebastian, and rubs his hands.

"'Ye have just compounded with rank treason-felony for the same bribe,' says Sir John. 'Wherefore to horse and get the guns.'

"But Master Collins meant the guns for Sir Andrew Barton all along, didn't he?" said Dan.

"Questionless, that he did," said Hal. "But he lost them. We poured into the village on the red edge of dawn, Sir John horsed, in half-armour, his pennon flying; behind him thirty stout Brightling knaves, five abreast; behind them four wool-wains, and behind them four trumpets to triumph over the jest, blowing: *Our King went forth to Normandie.* When we halted and rolled the ringing guns out of the tower, 'twas for all the world like Friar Roger's picture of the French siege in the Queen's Missal-book."

"And what did we – I mean, what did our village do?" said Dan.

"Oh! Bore it nobly – nobly," cried Hal. "Though they had tricked me, I was proud of them. They came out of their housen, looked at that little army as though it had been a post, and went their shut-mouthed way. Never a sign! Never a word! They'd ha' perished sooner than let Brightling overcrow us. Even that villain, Ticehurst Will, coming out of the Bell for his morning ale, he all but runs under Sir John's horse.

"'Ware, Sirrah Devil!' cries Sir John, reining back.

"'Oh!' says Will. 'Market day, is it? And all the bullocks from Brightling here?'

"I spared him his belting for that – the brazen knave!

"But John Collins was our masterpiece! He happened along-street (his jaw tied up where Sebastian had clouted him) when we were trundling the first demi-cannon through the lych-gate.

"'I reckon you'll find her middlin' heavy,' he says. 'If you've a mind to pay, I'll loan ye my timber-tug. She won't lie easy on ary wool-wain'

That was the one time I ever saw Sebastian taken flat aback. He opened and shut his mouth, fishy-like.

"'No offence,' says Master John. 'You've got her reason-

able good cheap. I thought ye might not grudge me a groat
if I helped move her." Ah, he was a masterpiece! They say
that morning's work cost our John two hundred pounds,
and he never winked an eyelid, not even when he saw the
guns all carted off to Lewes."

"Neither then nor later?" said Puck.

"Once. 'Twas after he gave St Barnabas' the new chime
of bells. (Oh, there was nothing the Collinses, or the Hayes,
or the Fowles, or the Penners would not do for the church
then! 'Ask and have' was their song.) We had rung 'em in,
and he was in the tower with Black Nick Fowle, that gave
us our rood-screen. The old man pinches the bell-rope one
hand and scratches his neck with t'other. "Sooner she was
pulling yon clapper than my neck," he says. That was all!
That was Sussex – seely Sussex for everlastin'!"

"And what happened after?" said Una.

"I went back into England," said Hal, slowly. "I'd had my
lesson against pride. But they tell me I left St Barnabas' a
jewel – just about a jewel! Well-a-well! 'Twas done for and
among my own people, and – Father Roger was right – I
never knew such trouble or such triumph since. That's the
nature o' things. A dear – dear land." He dropped his chin
on his chest.

"There's your Father at the Forge. What's he talking to
old Hobden about?" said Puck, opening his hand with three
leaves in it.

Dan looked towards the cottage.

"Oh, I know. It's that old oak lying across the brook.
Pater always wants it grubbed."

In the still valley they could hear old Hobden's deep
tones.

"Have it *as* you've a mind to," he was saying. "But the
vivers of her roots they hold the bank together. If you grub
her out, the bank she'll all come tearin' down, an' next
floods the brook'll swarve up. But have it *as* you've a mind.

The Mistuss she sets a heap by the ferns on her trunk."

"Oh! I'll think it over," said the Pater.

Una laughed a little bubbling chuckle.

"What Devil's in *that* belfry?" said Hal, with a lazy laugh. "That should be a Hobden by his voice."

"Why, the oak is the regular bridge for all the rabbits between the Three Acre and our meadow. The best place for wires on the farm, Hobden says. He's got two there now," Una answered. *"He* won't ever let it be grubbed!"

"Ah, Sussex! Seely Sussex for everlastin'," murmured Hal; and the next moment their Father's voice calling across to Little Lindens broke the spell as little St Barnabas' clock struck five.

A SMUGGLERS' SONG

If you wake at midnight, and hear a horse's feet,
Don't go drawing back the blind, or looking in the street,
Them that asks no questions isn't told a lie.
Watch the wall, my darling, while the Gentlemen go by!

> *Five-and-twenty ponies,*
> *Trotting through the dark*
> *Brandy for the Parson,*
> *'Baccy for the Clerk;*
> *Laces for a lady; letters for a spy,*

And watch the wall, my darling, while the Gentlemen go by!

Running round the woodlump if you chance to find
Little barrels, roped and tarred, all full of brandy wine;
Don't you shout to come and look, nor take 'em for your play;
Put the brishwood back again, – and they'll be gone next day!

If you see the stable door setting open wide;
If you see a tired horse lying down inside;
If your mother mends a coat cut about and tore;
If the lining's wet and warm – don't you ask no more!

If you meet King George's men, dressed in blue and red,
You be careful what you say, and mindful what is said.
If they call you "pretty maid," and chuck you 'neath the chin,
Don't you tell where no one is, nor yet where no one's been!

Knocks and footsteps round the house – whistles after dark –
You've no call for running out till the house-dogs bark.
Trusty's here, and Pincher's here, and see how dumb they lie –
They don't fret to follow when the Gentlemen go by!

If you do as you've been told, likely there's a chance
You'll be give a dainty doll, all the way from France,
With a cap of Valenciennes, and a velvet hood –
A present from the Gentlemen, along o' being good!

>   *Five-and-twenty ponies,*
>   *Trotting through the dark*
>   *Brandy for the Parson,*
>   *'Baccy for the Clerk.*

Them that asks no questions isn't told a lie –
Watch the wall, my darling, while the Gentlemen go by!

"Dymchurch Flit"

THE BEE BOY'S SONG

Bees! Bees! Hark to your bees!
"Hide from your neighbours as much as you please,
But all that has happened, to us you must tell,
Or else we will give you no honey to sell!"

A Maiden in her glory,
Upon her wedding-day,
Must tell her Bees the story,
Or else they'll fly away.
Fly away – die away –
Dwindle down and leave you!
But if you don't deceive your Bees,
Your Bees will not deceive you.

Marriage, birth or buryin',
News across the seas,
All you're sad or merry in,
You must tell the Bees.
Tell 'em coming in an' out,
Where the Fanners fan,
'Cause the Bees are justabout
As curious as a man!

Don't you wait where trees are,
When the lightnings play;
Nor don't you hate where Bees are
Or else they'll pine away.

Pine away – dwine away –
Anything to leave you!
But if you never grieve your Bees,
Your Bees'll never grieve you!

Just at dusk, a soft September rain began to fall on the hop-pickers. The mothers wheeled the bouncing perambulators out of the gardens; bins were put away, and tally-books made up. The young couples strolled home, two to each umbrella, and the single men walked behind them laughing. Dan and Una, who had been picking after their lessons, marched off to roast potatoes at the oast-house, where old Hobden, with Blue-eyed Bess, his lurcher dog, lived all the month through, drying the hops.

They settled themselves, as usual, on the sack-strewn cot in front of the fires, and, when Hobden drew up the shutter, stared, as usual, at the flameless bed of coals spouting its heat up the dark well of the old-fashioned roundel. Slowly he cracked off a few fresh pieces of coal, packed them, with fingers that never flinched, exactly where they would do most good; slowly he reached behind him till Dan tilted the potatoes into his iron scoop of a hand; carefully he arranged them round the fire, and then stood for a moment, black against the glare. As he closed the shutter, the oast-house seemed dark before the day's end, and he lit the candle in the lanthorn. The children liked all these things because they knew them so well.

The Bee Boy, Hobden's son, who is not quite right in his head, though he can do anything with bees, slipped in like a shadow. They only guessed it when Bess's stump-tail wagged against them.

A big voice began singing outside in the drizzle:

"Old Mother Laidinwool had nigh twelve months been dead,
She heard the hops were doin' well, and then popped up her
   head."

"There can't be two people made to holler like that!" cried old Hobden, wheeling round.

"'For,' says she, 'The boys I've picked with when I was young and fair,
They're bound to be at hoppin', and I'm – '"

A man showed at the doorway.

"Well, well! They do say hoppin'll draw the very deadest, and now I belief 'em. You, Tom? Tom Shoesmith?" Hobden lowered his lanthorn.

"You're a hem of a time makin' your mind to it, Ralph!" The stranger strode in – three full inches taller than Hobden, a grey-whiskered, brown-faced giant with clear blue eyes. They shook hands, and the children could hear the hard palms rasp together.

"You ain't lost none o' your grip," said Hobden. "Was it thirty or forty year back you broke my head at Peasmarsh Fair?"

"Only thirty, an' no odds 'tween us regardin' heads, neither. You had it back at me with a hop-pole. How did we get home that night? Swimmin'?"

"Same way the pheasant come into Gubbs's pocket – by a little luck an' a deal o' conjurin'." Old Hobden laughed in his deep chest.

"I see you've not forgot your way about the woods. D'ye do any o' *this* still?" The stranger pretended to look along a gun.

Hobden answered with a quick movement of the hand as though he were pegging down a rabbit wire.

"No. *That's* all that's left me now. Age she must as Age she can. An' what's your news since all these years."

"Oh, I've bin to Plymouth, I've bin to Dover –
I've bin ramblin', boys, the wide world over,"

the man answered cheerily. "I reckon I know as much of Old England as most." He turned towards the children and winked boldly.

"I lay they told you a sight o' lies, then. I've been into England fur as Wiltsheer once. I was cheated proper over a pair of hedgin'-gloves," said Hobden.

"There's fancy-talkin' everywhere. *You've* cleaved to your own parts pretty middlin' close, Ralph."

"Can't shift an old tree 'thout it dyin'," Hobden chuckled. "An' I be no more anxious to die than you look to be to help me with my hops tonight."

The great man leaned against the brickwork of the roundel, and swung his arms abroad. "Hire me!" was all he said, and they stumped upstairs laughing.

The children heard their shovels rasp on the cloth where the yellow hops lie drying above the fires, and all the oast-house filled with the sweet, sleepy smell as they were turned.

"Who is it?" Una whispered to the Bee Boy.

"Dunno, no more'n you – if *you* dunno," said he, and smiled.

The voices on the drying-floor talked and chuckled together, and the heavy footsteps moved back and forth. Presently a hop-pocket dropped through the press-hole overhead, and stiffened and fattened as they shovelled it full. "Clank!" went the press, and rammed the loose stuff into tight cake.

"Gentle!" they heard Hobden cry. "You'll bust her crop if you lay on so. You be as careless as Gleason's bull, Tom. Come an' sit by the fires. She'll do now."

They came down, and as Hobden opened the shutter to see if the potatoes were done Tom Shoesmith said to the children, "Put a plenty salt on 'em. That'll show you the sort o' man *I* be." Again he winked, and again the Bee Boy laughed and Una stared at Dan.

"*I* know what sort o' man you be," old Hobden grunted, groping for the potatoes round the fire.

"Do ye?" Tom went on behind his back. "Some of us can't abide Horseshoes, or Church Bells, or Running Water; an', talkin' o' runnin' water" – he turned to Hobden, who was backing out of the roundel – "d'you mind the great floods at Robertsbridge, when the miller's man was drowned in the street?"

"Middlin' well." Old Hobden let himself down on the coals by the fire-door. "I was courtin' my woman on the Marsh that year. Carter to Mus' Plum I was, gettin' ten shillin's week. Mine was a Marsh woman."

"Won'erful odd-gates place – Romney Marsh," said Tom Shoesmith. "I've heard say the world's divided like into Europe, Ashy, Afriky, Ameriky, Australy, an' Romney Marsh."

"The Marsh folk think so, said Hobden. "I had a hem o' trouble to get my woman to leave it."

"Where did she come out of? I've forgot, Ralph."

"Dymchurch under the Wall," Hobden answered, a potato in his hand.

"Then she'd be a Pett – or a Whitgift, would she?"

"Whitgift." Hobden broke open the potato and ate it with the curious neatness of men who make most of their meals in the blowy open. "She growed to be quite reasonable-like after livin' in the Weald awhile, but our first twenty year or two she was odd-fashioned, no bounds. And she was a won'erful hand with bees." He cut away a little piece of potato and threw it out to the door.

"Ah! I've heard say the Whitgifts could see further through a millstone than most," said Shoesmith. "Did she, now?"

"She was honest-innocent of any nigromancin'," said Hobden. "Only she'd read signs and sinnifications out o' birds flyin', stars fallin', bees hivin', and such. An' she'd lie awake – listenin' for calls, she said."

"That don't prove naught," said Tom. "All Marsh folk has been smugglers since time everlastin'. 'Twould be in her blood to listen out o' nights."

"Nature-ally," old Hobden replied, smiling. "I mind when there was smugglin' a sight nearer us than what the Marsh be. But that wasn't my woman's trouble. 'Twas a passel o' no-sense talk" – he dropped his voice – "about Pharisees."

"Yes. I've heard Marsh men belief in 'em." Tom looked straight at the wide-eyed children beside Bess.

"Pharisees," cried Una. "Fairies? Oh, *I* see!"

"People o' the Hills," said the Bee Boy, throwing half of his potato towards the door.

"There you be!" said Hobden, pointing at him. "My boy he has her eyes and her out-gate sense. That's what *she* called 'em!"

"And what did you think of it all?"

"Um – um," Hobden rumbled. "A man that uses fields an' shaws after dark as much as I've done, he don't go out of his road excep' for keepers."

"But settin' that aside?" said Tom, coaxingly. "I saw ye throw the Good Piece out-at-doors just now. Do ye believe or – *do* ye?"

"There was a great black eye to that tater," said Hobden indignantly.

"My liddle eye didn't see un, then. It looked as if you meant it for – for Any One that might need it. But settin' that aside, d'ye believe or – *do* ye?"

"I ain't sayin' nothin', because I've heard naught, an' I've see naught. But if you was to say there was more things after dark in the shaws than men, or fur, or feather, or fin, I dunno as I'd go far about to call you a liar. Now turn again, Tom. What's your say?"

"I'm like you. I say nothin'. But I'll tell you a tale, an' you can fit it *as* how you please."

"Passel o' no-sense stuff," growled Hobden, but he filled his pipe.

"The Marsh men they call it Dymchurch Flit," Tom went on slowly. "Hap you have heard it?"

"My woman she've told it me scores o' times. Dunno as I didn't end by belieftin' it – sometimes."

Hobden crossed over as he spoke, and sucked with his pipe at the yellow lanthorn flame. Tom rested one great elbow on one great knee, where he sat among the coal.

"Have you ever bin in the Marsh?" he said to Dan.

"Only as far as Rye, once," Dan answered.

"Ah, that's but the edge. Back behind of her there's steeples settin' beside churches, an' wise women settin' beside their doors, an' the sea settin' above the land, an' ducks herdin' wild in the diks" (he meant ditches). "The Marsh is just about riddled with diks an' sluices, an' tide-gates an' water-lets. You can hear 'em bubblin' an' grummelin' when the tide works in 'em, an' then you hear the sea rangin' left and right-handed all up along the Wall. You've seen how flat she is – the Marsh? You'd think nothin' easier than to walk eend-on acrost her? Ah, but the diks an' the water-lets, they twists the roads about as ravelly as witch-yarn on the spindles. So ye get all turned round in broad daylight."

"That's because they've dreened the waters into the diks," said Hobden. "When I courted my woman the rushes was green – Eh me! the rushes was green – an' the Bailiff o' the Marshes he rode up and down as free as the fog."

"Who was he?" said Dan.

"Why, the Marsh fever an' ague. He've clapped me on the shoulder once or twice till I shook proper. But now the dreenin' off of the waters have done away with the fevers; so they make a joke, like, that the Bailiff o' the Marshes broke his neck in a dik. A won'erful place for bees an' ducks 'tis too."

"An' old," Tom went on. "Flesh an' Blood have been there since Time Everlastin' Beyond. Well, now, speakin' among themselves, the Marsh men say that from Time Everlastin' Beyond, the Pharisees favoured the Marsh above the rest of Old England. I lay the Marsh men ought to know. They've been out after dark, father an' son, smugglin' some one thing or t'other, since ever wool grew to sheep's backs. They say there was always a middlin' few Pharisees to be seen on the Marsh. Impident as rabbits, they was. They'd dance on the nakid roads in the nakid daytime; they'd flash their liddle green lights along the diks, comin' an' goin', like honest smugglers. Yes, an' times they'd lock the church doors against parson an' clerk of Sundays."

"That 'ud be smugglers layin' in the lace or the brandy till they could run it out o' the Marsh. I've told my woman so," said Hobden.

"I'll lay she didn't belieft it, then – not if she was a Whitgift. A won'erful choice place for Pharisees, the Marsh, by all accounts, till Queen Bess's father he come in with his Reformatories."

"Would that be a Act of Parliament like?" Hobden asked.

"Sure-ly. Can't do nothing in Old England without Act, Warrant an' Summons. He got his Act allowed him, an', they say, Queen Bess's father he used the parish churches something shameful. Just about tore the gizzards out of I dunnamany. Some folk in England they held with 'en; but some they saw it different, an' it eended in 'em takin' sides an' burnin' each other no bounds, accordin' which side was top, time bein'. That tarrified the Pharisees: for Goodwill among Flesh an' Blood is meat an' drink to 'em, an' ill-will is poison."

"Same as bees," said the Bee Boy. "Bees won't stay by a house where there's hating."

"True," said Tom. "This Reformatories tarrified the Pharisees same as the reaper goin' round a last stand o' wheat tarrifies rabbits. They packed into the Marsh from all parts, and they says, "Fair or foul, we must flit out o' this, for Merry England's done with, an' we're reckoned among the Images.'"

"Did they *all* see it that way?" said Hobden.

"All but one that was called Robin – if you've heard of, him. What are you laughin' at?" Tom turned to Dan. "The Pharisees's trouble didn't tech Robin, because he'd cleaved middlin' close to people, like. No more he never meant to go out of Old England – not he; so he was sent messagin' for help among Flesh an' Blood. But Flesh an' Blood must always think of their own concerns, an' Robin couldn't get *through* at 'em, ye see. They thought it was tide-echoes off the Marsh."

"What did you – what did the fai – Pharisees want?" Una asked.

"A boat, to be sure. Their liddle wings could no more cross Channel than so many tired butterflies. A boat an' a crew they desired to sail 'em over to France, where yet awhile folks hadn't tore down the Images. They couldn't abide cruel Canterbury Bells ringin' to Bulverhithe for more pore men an' women to be burnded, nor the King's proud messenger ridin' through the land givin' orders to tear down the Images. They couldn't abide it no shape Nor yet they couldn't get their boat an' crew to flit by without Leave an' Good-will from Flesh an' Blood; an' Flesh an' Blood came an' went about its own business the while the Marsh was swarvin' up, an' swarvin' up with Pharisees from all England over, strivin' all means to get *through* at Flesh an' Blood to tell 'em their sore need . . . I don't know as you've ever heard say Pharisees are like chickens?"

"My woman used to say that too," said Hobden, folding his brown arms.

"They be. You run too many chickens together, an' the ground sickens, like, an' you get a squat, an' your chickens die. Same way, you crowd Pharisees all in one place – *they* don't die, but Flesh an' Blood walkin' among 'em is apt to sick up an' pine off. *They* don't mean it, an' Flesh an' Blood don't know it, but that's the truth – as I've heard. The Pharisees through bein' all stenched up an' frighted, an' trying' to come *through* with their supplications, they nature-ally changed the thin airs an' humours in Flesh an' Blood. It lay on the Marsh like thunder. Men saw their churches ablaze with the wildfire in the windows after dark; they saw their cattle scatterin' an' no man scarin'; their sheep flockin' an' no man drivin'; their horses latherin' an' no man leadin'; they saw the liddle low green lights more than ever in the dik-sides; they heard the liddle feet patterin' more than ever round the houses; an' night an' day, day an' night, 'twas all as though they were bein' creeped up on, an' hinted at by Some One or other that couldn't rightly shape their trouble. Oh, I lay they sweated! Man an' maid, woman an' child, their nature done 'em no service all the weeks while the Marsh was swarvin' up with Pharisees. But they was Flesh an' Blood, an' Marsh men before all. They reckoned the signs sinnified trouble for the Marsh. Or that the sea 'ud rear up against Dymchurch Wall an' they'd be drownded like Old Winchelsea; or that the Plague was comin'. So they looked for the meanin' in the sea or in the clouds – far an' high up. They never thought to look near an' knee-high, where they could see naught.

"Now there was a poor widow at Dymchurch under the Wall, which, lacking man or property, she had the more time for feeling; and she come to feel there was a Trouble outside her doorstep bigger an' heavier than aught she'd ever carried over it. She had two sons – one born blind, an' t'other struck dumb through fallin' off the Wall when he was liddle. They was men grown, but not wage earnin', an' she worked for 'em, keepin' bees and answerin' Questions."

"What sort of questions?" said Dan.

"Like where lost things might be found, an' what to put about a crooked baby's neck, an' how to join parted sweethearts. She felt the Trouble on the Marsh same as eels feel thunder. She was a wise woman."

"My woman was won'erful weather-tender, too," said Hobden. "I've seen her brish sparks like off an anvil out of her hair in thunderstorms. But she never laid out to answer Questions."

"This woman was a Seeker, like, an' Seekers they sometimes find. One night, while she lay abed, hot an' achin', there come a Dream an' tapped at her window, an' 'Widow Whitgift,' it said, 'Widow Whitgift!'

"First, by the wings an' the whistlin', she thought it was peewits, but last she arose an' dressed herself, an' opened her door to the Marsh, an' she felt the Trouble an' the Groanin' all about her, strong as fever an' ague, arl' she calls: 'What is it? Oh, what is it?'

"Then 'twas all like the frogs in the diks peepin': then 'twas all like the reeds in the diks clip-clappin'; an' then the great Tide-wave rummelled along the Wall, an' she couldn't hear proper.

"Three times she called, an' three times the Tide-wave did her down. But she catched the quiet between, an' she cries out, 'What is the Trouble on the Marsh that's been lying down with my heart an' arising with my body this month gone?' She felt a liddle hand lay hold on her gown-hem, an' she stooped to the pull o' that liddle hand."

Tom Shoesmith spread his huge fist before the fire and smiled at it as he went on.

"'Will the sea drown the Marsh?' she says. She was a Marsh woman first an' foremost.

"'No,' says the liddle voice. 'Sleep sound for all o' that.'

"'Is the Plague comin' to the Marsh?' she says. Them was all the ills she knowed.

"'No. Sleep sound for all o' that,' says Robin.

"She turned about, half mindful to go in, but the liddle voices grieved that shrill an' sorrowful she turns back, an' she cries: 'If it is not a Trouble of Flesh an' Blood, what can I do?'

"The Pharisees cried out upon her from all round to fetch them a boat to sail to France, an' come back no more.

"'There's a boat on the Wall,' she says, 'but I can't push it down to the sea, nor sail it when 'tis there.'

"'Lend us your sons,' says all the Pharisees. 'Give 'em Leave an' Goodwill to sail it for us, Mother – O Mother!'

"'One's dumb, an' t'other's blind,' she says. 'But all the dearer me for that; and you'll lose them in the big sea.' The voices just about pierced through her; an' there was children's voices too. She stood out all she could, but she couldn't rightly stand against *that*. So she says: 'If you can draw my sons for your job, I'll not hinder 'em. You can't ask no more of a Mother.'

"She saw them liddle green lights dance an' cross till she was dizzy; she heard them liddle feet patterin' by the thousand; she heard cruel Canterbury Bells ringing to Bulverhithe, an' she heard the great Tide wave ranging along the Wall. That was while the Pharisees was workin' a Dream to wake her two sons asleep: an' while she bit on her fingers she saw them two she'd bore come out an' pass her with never a word. She followed 'em, cryin' pitiful, to the old boat on the Wall, an' that they took an' runned down to the sea.

"When they'd stepped mast an' sail the blind son speaks: 'Mother, we're waitin' your Leave an' Goodwill to take Them over.'"

Tom Shoesmith threw back his head and half shut his eyes.

"Eh, me!" he said. "She was a fine, valiant woman, the Widow Whitgift. She stood twistin' the eends of her long hair over her fingers, an' she shook like a poplar, makin' up her mind. The Pharisees all about they hushed their children from cryin' an' they waited dumb-still. She was all their dependence. 'Thout her Leave an' Goodwill they could not pass; for she was the Mother. So she shook like a aps tree makin' up her mind. Last she drives the word past her teeth, an' 'Go!' she says. 'Go with my Leave an' Goodwill.'

"Then I saw – then, they say, she had to brace back same as if she was wadin' in tide-water; for the Pharisees just about flowed past her – down the beach to the boat, I dunnamany of 'em – with their wives an' childern an' valooables, all escapin' out of cruel Old England. Silver you could hear clinkin', an' liddle bundles hove down dunt on the bottom-boards, an' passels o' liddle swords an' shields raklin', an' liddle fingers an' toes scratchin' on the boatside to board her when the two sons pushed her off. That boat she sunk lower an' lower, but all the Widow could see in it was her boys movin' hampered-like to get at the tackle. Up sail they did, an' away they went, deep as a Rye barge, away into the off-shore mistës, an' the Widow Whitgift she sat down an' eased her grief till mornin' light."

"I never heard she was *all* alone," said Hobden.

"I remember now. The one called Robin he stayed with her, they tell. She was all too grievious to listen to his promises."

"Ah! She should ha' made her bargain beforehand. I allus told my woman so!" Hobden cried.

"No. She loaned her sons for a pure love-loan, bein' as she sensed the Trouble on the Marshes, an' was simple good-willin' to ease it." Tom laughed softly. "She done that. Yes, she done that! From Hithe to Bulverhithe, fretty man an' maid, ailin' woman an' wailin' child, they took the advantage of the change in the thin airs just about *as* soon as the Pharisees flitted. Folks come out fresh an' shinin' all over the Marsh like snails after wet. An' that while the

Widow Whitgift sat grievin' on the Wall. She might have belieft us – she might have trusted her sons would be sent back! She fussed, no bounds, when their boat come in after three days."

"And, of course, the sons were both quite cured?" said Una.

"No-o. That would have been out o' nature. She got 'em back *as* she sent 'em. The blind man he hadn't seen naught of anythin', an' the dumb man nature-ally he couldn't say aught of what he'd seen. I reckon that was why the Pharisees pitched on 'em for the ferryin' job."

"But what did you – what did Robin promise the Widow?" said Dan.

"What *did* he promise, now?" Tom pretended to think. "Wasn't your woman a Whitgift, Ralph? Didn't she ever say?"

"She told me a passel o' no-sense stuff when he was born." Hobden pointed at his son. "There was always to be one of 'em that could see further into a millstone than most."

"Me! That's me!" said the Bee Boy so suddenly that they all laughed.

"I've got it now!" cried Tom, slapping his knee. "So long as Whitgift blood lasted, Robin promised there would allers be one o' her stock that – that no Trouble 'ud lie on, no Maid 'ud sigh on, no Night could frighten, no Fright could harm, no Harm could make sin, an' no Woman could make a fool of."

"Well, ain't that just me?" said the Bee Boy, where he sat in the silver square of the great September moon that was staring into the oast-house door.

"They was the exact words she told me when we first found he wasn't like others. But it beats me how you known 'em," said Hobden.

"Aha! There's more under my hat besides hair?" Tom

laughed and stretched himself. "When I've seen these two young folk home, we'll make a night of old days, Ralph, with passin' old tales – eh? An' where might you live?" he said, gravely, to Dan. "An' do you think your Pa 'ud give me a drink for takin' you there, Missy?"

They giggled so at this that they had to run out. Tom picked them both up, set one on each broad shoulder, and tramped across the ferny pasture where the cows puffed milky puffs at them in the moonlight.

"Oh, Puck! Puck! I guessed you right from when you talked about the salt. How could you ever do it?" Una cried, swinging along delighted.

"Do what?" he said, and climbed the stile by the pollard oak.

"Pretend to be Tom Shoesmith," said Dan, and they ducked to avoid the two little ashes that grow by the bridge over the brook. Tom was almost running.

"Yes. That's my name, Mus' Dan," he said, hurrying over the silent shining lawn, where a rabbit sat by the big white-thorn near the croquet ground. "Here you be." He strode into the old kitchen yard, and slid them down as Ellen came to ask questions.

"I'm helping in Mus' Spray's oast-house," he said to her. "No, I'm no foreigner. I knowed this country 'fore your mother was born; an' – yes, it's dry work oastin', Miss. Thank you."

Ellen went to get a jug, and the children went in magicked once more by Oak, Ash and Thorn!

A THREE-PART SONG

> I'm just in love with all these three,
> The Weald an' the Marsh an' the Down countrie;
> Nor I don't know which I love the most,
> The Weald or the Marsh or the white chalk coast!

I've buried my heart in a ferny hill,
Twix' a liddle low shaw an' a great high gill.
Oh, hop-bine yaller an' wood-smoke blue,
I reckon you'll keep her middling true!

I've loosed my mind for to out an' run
On a Marsh that was old when Kings begun:
Oh, Romney level an' Brenzett reeds,
I reckon you know what my mind needs!

I've given my soul to the Southdown grass,
An' sheep-bells tinkled where you pass.
Oh, Firle an' Ditchling an' sails at sea,
I reckon you keep my soul for me!

The Treasure and the Law

When first by Eden Tree
The Four Great Rivers ran,
To each was appointed a Man
Her Prince and Ruler to be.

But after this was ordained,
(The ancient legends tell),
There came dark Israel,
For whom no River remained.

Then He That is Wholly Just
Said to him: "Fling on the ground
A handful of yellow dust,
And a Fifth Great River shall run,
Mightier than these four,
In secret the Earth around;
And Her secret evermore
Shall be shown to thee and thy Race.

So it was said and done.
And, deep in the veins of Earth,
And, fed by a thousand springs
That comfort the market-place,
Or sap the power of Kings,
The Fifth Great River had birth,
Even as it was foretold –
The Secret River of Gold!

And Israel laid down
His sceptre and his crown,
To brood on that River bank,
Where the waters flashed and sank,
And burrowed in earth and fell,
And bided a season below;
For reason that none might know,
Save only Israel.

He is Lord of the Last
The Fifth, most wonderful, Flood.
He hears Her thunder past
And Her song is in his blood.
He can foresay: "She will fall,"
For he knows which fountain dries
Behind which desert-belt
A thousand leagues to the South.
He can foresay: "She will rise."
He knows what far snows melt
Along what mountain-wall
A thousand leagues to the North.
He snuffs the coming drouth
As he snuffs the coming rain,
He knows what each will bring forth,
And turns it to his gain.

A Prince without a Sword,
A Ruler without a Throne;
Israel follows his quest.
In every land a guest,
Of many lands a lord,
In no land King is he.
But the Fifth Great River keeps
The secret of Her deeps
For Israel alone,
As it was ordered to be.

Now it was the third week in November, and the woods rang
with the noise of pheasant-shooting. No one hunted that steep,
cramped country except the village beagles, who, as often as
not, escaped from their kennels and made a day of their own.
Dan and Una found a couple of them towling round the
kitchen-garden after the laundry cat. The little brutes were
only too pleased to go rabbiting, so the children ran them all
along the brook pastures and into Little Lindens farmyard,
where the old sow vanquished them – and up to the quarry-
hole, where they started a fox. He headed for Far Wood, and
there they frightened out all the pheasants, who were shelter-
ing from a big beat across the valley. Then the cruel guns began again, and they grabbed the beagles lest they should stray
and get hurt.

"I wouldn't be a pheasant – in November – for a lot," Dan
panted, as he caught Folly by the neck. "Why did you laugh
that horrid way?"

"I didn't," said Una, sitting on Flora, the fat lady-dog.
"Oh, look! The silly birds are going back to their own
woods instead of ours, where they would be safe."

"Safe till it pleased you to kill them." An old man, so tall
he was almost a giant, stepped from behind the clump of
hollies by Volaterrae. The children jumped, and the dogs
dropped like setters. He wore a sweeping gown of dark
thick stuff, lined and edged with yellowish fur, and he
bowed a bent-down bow that made them feel both proud
and ashamed. Then he looked at them steadily, and they
stared back without doubt or fear.

"You are not afraid?" he said, running his hands through
his splendid grey beard. "Not afraid that those men yonder"
– he jerked his head towards the incessant pop-pop of the
guns from the lower woods – "will do you hurt?"

"We-ell" – Dan liked to be accurate, especially when he
was shy – "old Hobd – a friend of mine told me that one of
the beaters got peppered last week – hit in the leg, I mean.

You see, Mr Meyer *will* fire at rabbits. But he gave Waxy Garnett a quid – sovereign, I mean – and Waxy told Hobden he'd have stood both barrels for half the money."

"He doesn't understand," Una cried, watching the pale, troubled face. "Oh, I wish – ."

She had scarcely said it when Puck rustled out of the hollies and spoke to the man quickly in foreign words. Puck wore a long cloak too – the afternoon was just frosting down – and it changed his appearance altogether.

"Nay, nay!" he said at last. "You did not understand the boy. A freeman was a little hurt, by pure mischance, at the hunting."

"I know that mischance! What did his lord do? Laugh and ride over him?" the old man sneered.

"It was one of your own people did the hurt, Kadmiel." Puck's eyes twinkled maliciously. "So he gave the freeman a piece of gold, and no more was said."

"A Jew drew blood from a Christian and no more was said?" Kadmiel cried. "Never! When did they torture him?"

"No man may be bound, or fined, or slain till he has been judged by his peers," Puck insisted. "There is but one Law in Old England for Jew or Christian – the Law that was signed at Runnymede."

"Why, that's Magna Charta!" Dan whispered. It was one of the few history dates that he could remember.

Kadmiel turned on him with a sweep and a whirr of his spicy-scented gown.

"Dost *thou* know of that, babe?" he cried, and lifted his hands in wonder.

"Yes," said Dan firmly.

> "Magna Charta was signed by John,
> That Henry the Third put his heel upon.

"And old Hobden says that if it hadn't been for *her* (he calls everything "her", you know), the keepers would have him clapped in Lewes Jail all the year round."

Again Puck translated to Kadmiel in the strange, solemn-sounding language, and at last Kadmiel laughed .

"Out of the mouths of babes do we learn," said he. "But tell me now, and I will not call you a babe but a Rabbi, *why* did the King sign the roll of the New Law at Runnymede? For he was a King."

Dan looked sideways at his sister. It was her turn.

"Because he jolly well had to," said Una softly. "The Barons made him."

"Nay," Kadmiel answered, shaking his head. "You Christians always forget that gold does more than the sword. Our good King signed because he could not borrow more money from us bad Jews." He curved his shoulders as he spoke. "A King without gold is a snake with a broken back, and" – his nose sneered up and his eyebrows frowned down – "it is a good deed to break a snake's back. That was my work," he cried, triumphantly, to Puck. "Spirit of Earth, bear witness that that was *my* work!" He shot up to his full towering height, and his words rang like a trumpet. He had a voice that changed its tone almost as an opal changes colour – sometimes deep and thundery, sometimes thin and waily, but always it made you listen.

"Many people can bear witness to that," Puck answered. "Tell these babes how it was done. Remember, Master, they do not know Doubt or Fear."

"So I saw in their faces when we met," said Kadmiel. "Yet surely, surely they are taught to spit upon Jews?"

"Are they?" said Dan, much interested. "Where at?"

Puck fell back a pace, laughing. "Kadmiel is thinking of King John's reign," he explained. "His people were badly treated then."

"Oh, we know *that*," they answered, and (it was very rude of them, but they could not help it) they stared straight at Kadmiel's mouth to see if his teeth were all there. It stuck in their lesson-memory that King John used to pull out Jews' teeth to make them lend him money.

Kadmiel understood the look and smiled bitterly.

"No. Your King never drew my teeth: I think, perhaps, I drew his. Listen! I was not born among Christians, but among Moors – in Spain – in a little white town under the mountains. Yes, the Moors are cruel, but at least their learned men dare to think. It was prophesied of me at my birth that I should be a Lawgiver to a People of a strange speech and a hard language. We Jews are always looking for the Prince and the Lawgiver to come. Why not? My people in the town (we were very few) set me apart as a child of the prophecy – the Chosen of the Chosen. We Jews dream so many dreams. You would never guess it to see us slink about the rubbish-heaps in our quarter; but at the day's end – doors shut, candles lit – aha! *then* we became the Chosen again."

He paced back and forth through the wood as he talked. The rattle of the shot-guns never ceased, and the dogs whimpered a little and lay flat on the leaves.

"I was a Prince. Yes! Think of a little Prince who had never known rough words in his own house handed over to shouting, bearded Rabbis, who pulled his ears and filliped his nose, all that he might learn – learn – learn to be King when his time came. Hé! Such a little Prince it was! One eye he kept on the stone-throwing Moorish boys, and the other it roved about the streets looking for his Kingdom. Yes, and he learned to cry softly when he was hunted up and down those streets. He learned to do all things without noise. He played beneath his father's table when the Great Candle was lit, and he listened as children listen to the talk of his father's friends above the table. They came across the mountains, from out of all the world, for my Prince's father was their counsellor. They came from behind the armies of

Sala-ud-Din: from Rome: from Venice: from England. They stole down our alley, they tapped secretly at our door, they took off their rags, they arrayed themselves, and they talked to my father at the wine. All over the world the heathen fought each other. They brought news of these wars, and while he played beneath the table, my Prince heard these meanly dressed ones decide between themselves how, and when, and for how long King should draw sword against King, and People rise up against People. Why not? There can be no war without gold, and we Jews know how the earth's gold moves with the seasons, and the crops, and the winds; circling and looping and rising and sinking away like a river a wonderful underground river. How should the foolish Kings know *that* while they fight and steal and kill?"

The children's faces showed that they knew nothing at all as, with open eyes, they trotted and turned beside the long-striding old man. He twitched his gown over his shoulders, and a square plate of gold, studded with jewels, gleamed for an instant through the fur, like a star through flying snow.

"No matter," he said. "But, credit me, my Prince saw peace or war decided not once, but many times, by the fall of a coin spun between a Jew from Bury and a Jewess from Alexandria, in his father's house, when the Great Candle was lit. Such power had we Jews among the Gentiles. Ah, my little Prince! Do you wonder that he learned quickly? Why not?" He muttered to himself and went on: –

"My trade was that of a physician. When I had learned it in Spain I went to the East to find my Kingdom. Why not? A Jew is as free as a sparrow – or a dog. He goes where he is hunted. In the East I found libraries where men dared to think – schools of medicine where they dared to learn. I was diligent in my business. Therefore I stood before Kings. I have been a brother to Princes and a companion to beggars, and I have walked between the living and the dead. There was no profit in it. I did not find my Kingdom.

So, in the tenth year of my travels, when I had reached the Uttermost Eastern Sea, I returned to my father's house. God had wonderfully preserved my people. None had been slain, none even wounded, and only a few scourged. I became once more a son in my father's house. Again the Great Candle was lit; again the meanly apparelled ones tapped on our door after dusk; and again I heard them weigh out peace and war, as they weighed out the gold on the table. But I was not rich – not very rich. Therefore, when those that had power and knowledge and wealth talked together, I sat in the shadow. Why not?

"Yet all my wanderings had shown me one sure thing, which is, that a King without money is like a spear without a head. He cannot do much harm. I said, therefore, to Elias of Bury, a great one among our people: 'Why do our people lend any more to the Kings that oppress us?' 'Because,' said Elias, 'if we refuse they stir up their people against us, and the People are tenfold more cruel than Kings. If thou doubtest, come with me to Bury in England and live as I live.'

"I saw my mother's face across the candle flame, and I said, 'I will come with thee to Bury. Maybe my Kingdom shall be there.'

"So I sailed with Elias to the darkness and the cruelty of Bury in England, where there are no learned men. How can a man be wise if he hate? At Bury I kept his accounts for Elias, and I saw men kill Jews there by the tower. No one laid hands on Elias. He lent money to the King, and the King's favour was about him. A King will not take the life so long as there is any gold. This King – yes, John – oppressed his people bitterly because they would not give him money. Yet his land was a good land. If he had only given it rest he might have cropped it as a Christian crops his beard. But even *that* little he did not know, for God had deprived him of all understanding, and had multiplied pestilence, and famine, and despair upon the people. Therefore his people turned against us Jews, who are all people's dogs. Why not? Lastly the Barons and the people rose together against the King because of his cruelties. Nay – nay – the Barons did not love the people, but they saw that if the King cut up and destroyed the common people, he would presently destroy the Barons. They joined then, as cats and pigs will join to slay a snake. I kept the accounts, and I watched all these things, for I remembered the Prophecy.

"A great gathering of Barons (to most of whom we had lent money) came to Bury, and there, after much talk and a thousand runnings-about, they made a roll of the New Laws that they would force on the King. If he swore to keep those Laws, they would allow him a little money. That was the King's God – Money – to waste. They showed us the roll of the New Laws. Why not? We had lent them money. We knew all their counsels – we Jews shivering behind our doors in Bury." He threw out his hands suddenly. "We did not seek to be paid *all* in money. We sought Power – Power – Power! That is *our* God in our captivity. Power to use!

"I said to Elias: 'These New Laws are good. Lend no more money to the King: so long as he has money he will lie and slay the people.'

"'Nay,' said Elias. 'I know this people. They are madly cruel. Better one King than a thousand butchers. I have lent a little money to the Barons, or they would torture us, but my most I will lend to the King. He hath promised me a place near him at Court, where my wife and I shall be safe.'

"'But if the King be made to keep these New Laws,' I said, 'the land will have peace, and our trade will grow. If we lend he will fight again.'

"'Who made thee a Lawgiver in England?' said Elias.

"'*I* know this people. Let the dogs tear one another! I will lend the King ten thousand pieces of gold, and he can fight the Barons at his pleasure.'

"'There are not two thousand pieces of gold in all England this summer,' I said, for I kept the accounts, and I knew how the earth's gold moved – that wonderful underground river. Elias barred home the windows, and, his hands about his mouth, he told me how, when he was trading with small wares in a French ship, he had come to the Castle of Pevensey."

"Oh!" said Dan. "Pevensey again!" and looked at Una, who nodded and skipped.

"There, after they had scattered his pack up and down the Great Hall, some young knights carried him to an upper room, and dropped him into a well in a wall, that rose and fell with the tide. They called him Joseph, and threw torches at his wet head. Why not?"

"Why, of course!" cried Dan. "Didn't you know it was – ' Puck held up his hand to stop him, and Kadmiel, who never noticed, went on.

"When the tide dropped he thought he stood on old armour, but feeling with his toes, he raked up bar on bar of soft gold. Some wicked treasure of the old days put away, and the secret cut off by the sword. I have heard the like before."

"So have we," Una whispered. "But it wasn't wicked a bit."

"Elias took a little of the stuff with him, and thrice yearly he would return to Pevensey as a chapman, selling at no price or profit, till they suffered him to sleep in the empty room, where he would plumb and grope, and steal away a few bars. The great store of it still remained, and by long brooding he had come to look on it as his own. Yet when we thought how we should lift and convey it, we saw no way. This was before the Word of the Lord had come to me. A walled fortress possessed by Normans; in the midst a forty-foot-tide well out of which to remove secretly many horseloads of gold! Hopeless! So Elias wept. Adah, his wife, wept too. She had hoped to stand beside the Queen's Christian tiring-maids at Court, when the King should give them that place at Court which he had promised. Why not? She was born in England – an odious woman.

"The present evil to us was that Elias, out of his strong folly, had, as it were, promised the King that he would arm him with more gold. Wherefore the King in his camp stopped his ears against the Barons and the people. Wherefore men died daily. Adah so desired her place at Court, she besought Elias to tell the King where the treasure lay, that the King might take it by force, and they would trust in his gratitude. Why not? This Elias refused to do, for he looked on the gold as his own. They quarrelled, and they wept at the evening meal, and late in the night came one Langton – a priest, almost learned – to borrow more money for the Barons. Elias and Adah went to their chamber."

Kadmiel laughed scornfully in his beard. The shots across the valley stopped as the shooting party changed their ground for the last beat.

"So it was I, not Elias," he went on quietly, "that made terms with Langton touching the fortieth of the New Laws."

"What terms?" said Puck quickly. "The Fortieth of the Great Charter says: 'To none will we sell, refuse, or delay right or justice.'"

"True, but the Barons had written first: *To no free man*. It cost me two hundred broad pieces of gold to change those narrow words. Langton, the priest, understood. 'Jew though thou art,' said he, 'the change is just, and if ever Christian and Jew came to be equal in England thy people may thank thee.' Then he went out stealthily, as men do who deal with Israel by night. I think he spent my gift upon his altar. Why not? I have spoken with Langton. He was such a man as I might have been if – if we Jews had been a people. But yet, in many things, a child.

"I heard Elias and Adah abovestairs quarrel, and, knowing the woman was the stronger, I saw that Elias would tell the King of the gold and that the King would continue in his stubbornness. Therefore I saw that the gold must be put away from the reach of any man. Of a sudden, the Word of the Lord came to me saying, 'The Morning is come, O thou that dwellest in the land.'"

Kadmiel halted, all black against the pale green sky beyond the wood – a huge robed figure, like the Moses in the picture-Bible.

"I rose. I went out, and as I shut the door on that House of Foolishness, the woman looked from the window and whispered, 'I have prevailed on my husband to tell the King!' I answered: 'There is no need. The Lord is with me.'

"In that hour the Lord gave me full understanding of all that I must do; and His Hand covered me in my ways. First I went to London, to a physician of our people, who sold me certain drugs that I needed. You shall see why. Thence I went swiftly to Pevensey. Men fought all around me, for there were neither rulers nor judges in the abominable land. Yet when I walked by them they cried out that I was one Ahasuerus, a Jew, condemned, as they believe, to live for ever, and they fled from me everyways. Thus the Lord saved me for my work, and at Pevensey I bought me a little boat and moored it on the mud beneath the Marsh-gate of the Castle. That also God showed me."

He was as calm as though he were speaking of some stranger, and his voice filled the little bare wood with rolling music.

"I cast" – his hand went to his breast, and again the strange jewel gleamed – "I cast the drugs which I had prepared into the common well of the Castle. Nay, I did no harm. The more we physicians know, the less do we do. Only the fool says: 'I dare.' I caused a blotched and itching rash to break out upon their skins, but I knew it would fade in fifteen days. I did not stretch out my hand against their life. They in the Castle thought it was the Plague, and they ran out, taking with them their very dogs.

"A Christian physician, seeing that I was a Jew and a stranger, vowed that I had brought the sickness from London. This is the one time I have ever heard a Christian leech speak truth of any disease. Thereupon the people beat me, but a merciful woman said: 'Do not kill him now. Push him into our Castle with his Plague, and if, as he says, it will abate on the fifteenth day, we can kill him then.' Why not? They drove me across the drawbridge of the Castle, and fled back to their booths. Thus I came to be alone with the treasure."

"But did you know this was all going to happen just right?" said Una.

"My Prophecy was that I should be a Lawgiver to a People of a strange land and a hard speech. I knew I should not die. I washed my cuts. I found the tide-well in the wall, and from Sabbath to Sabbath I dove and dug there in that empty, Christian-smelling fortress. Hé! I spoiled the Egyptians! Hé! If they had only known! I drew up many good loads of gold, which I loaded by night into my boat. There had been gold dust too, but that had been washed out by the tides."

"Didn't you ever wonder who had put it there?" said Dan, stealing a glance at Puck's calm, dark face under the hood of his gown. Puck shook his head and pursed his lips.

"Often; for the gold was new to me," Kadmiel replied. "I know the Golds. I can judge them in the dark; but this was heavier and redder than any we deal in. Perhaps it was the very gold of Parvaim. Eh, why not? It went to my heart to heave it on to the mud, but I saw well that if the evil thing remained, or if even the hope of finding it remained, the King would not sign the New Laws, and the land would perish."

"Oh, Marvel!" said Puck, beneath his breath, rustling in the dead leaves.

"When the boat was loaded I washed my hands seven times, and pared beneath my nails, for I would not keep one grain. I went out by the little gate where the Castle's refuse is thrown. I dared not hoist sail lest men should see me; but the Lord commanded the tide to bear me carefully, and I was far from land before the morning."

"Weren't you afraid?" said Una.

"Why? There were no Christians in the boat. At sunrise I made my prayer, and cast the gold – all – all that gold into the deep sea! A King's ransom – no, the ransom of a People! When I had loosed hold of the last bar, the Lord commanded the tide to return me to a haven at the mouth of a river, and thence I walked across a wilderness to Lewes, where I have brethren. They opened the door to me, and they say – I had not eaten for two days – they say that I fell across the threshold, crying: 'I have sunk an army with horsemen in the sea!'"

"But you hadn't," said Una. "Oh, yes! I see! You meant that King John might have spent it on that?"

"Even so," said Kadmiel.

The firing broke out again close behind them. The pheasants poured over the top of a belt of tall firs. They could see young Mr Meyer, in his new yellow gaiters, very busy and excited at the end of the line, and they could hear the thud of the falling birds.

"But what did Elias of Bury do?" Puck demanded. "He had promised money to the King."

Kadmiel smiled grimly. "I sent him word from London that the Lord was on my side. When he heard that the Plague had broken out in Pevensey, and that a Jew had been thrust into the Castle to cure it, he understood my word was true. He and Adah hurried to Lewes and asked me for an accounting. He still looked on the gold as his own. I told them where I had laid it, and I gave them full leave to pick it up . . . Eh, well! The curses of a fool and the dust of a journey are two things no wise man can escape . . . But I pitied Elias! The King was wroth with him because he could not lend; the Barons were wroth too because they heard that he would have lent to the King; and Adah was wroth with him because she was an odious woman. They took ship from Lewes to Spain. That was wise!"

"And you? Did you see the signing of the Law at Runnymede?" said Puck, as Kadmiel laughed noiselessly.

"Nay. Who am I to meddle with things too high for me? I returned to Bury, and lent money on the autumn crops. Why not?"

There was a crackle overhead. A cock-pheasant that had sheered aside after being hit spattered down almost on top of them, driving up the dry leaves like a shell. Flora and Folly threw themselves at it; the children rushed forward, and when they had beaten them off and smoothed down the plumage Kadmiel had disappeared.

"Well," said Puck calmly, "what did you think of it? Weland gave the Sword! The Sword gave the Treasure, and the Treasure gave the Law. It's as natural as an oak growing.

"I don't understand. Didn't he know it was Sir Richard's old treasure?" said Dan. "And why did Sir Richard and Brother Hugh leave it lying about? And – and –"

"Never mind," said Una politely. "He'll let us come and go and look and know another time. Won't you, Puck?"

"Another time maybe," Puck answered. "Brr! It's cold and late. I'll race you towards home!"

They hurried down into the sheltered valley. The sun had almost sunk behind Cherry Clack, the trodden ground by the cattle-gates was freezing at the edges, and the new-waked north wind blew the night on them from over the hills. They picked up their feet and flew across the browned pastures, and when they halted, panting in the steam of their own breath the dead leaves whirled up behind them. There was Oak and Ash and Thorn enough in that year-end shower to magic away a thousand memories.

So they trotted to the brook at the bottom of the lawn, wondering why Flora and Folly had missed the quarry-hole fox.

Old Hobden was just finishing some hedge-work. They saw his white smock glimmer in the twilight where he faggoted the rubbish.

"Winter, he's come, I reckon, Mus' Dan," he called. "Hard times now till Heffle Cuckoo Fair. Yes, we'll all be glad to see the Old Woman let the Cuckoo out o' the basket for to start lawful Spring in England."

They heard a crash, and a stamp and a splash of water as though a heavy old cow were crossing almost under their noses.

Hobden ran forward angrily to the ford.

"Gleason's bull again, playin' Robin all over the Farm! Oh, look, Mus' Dan – his great footmark as big as a trencher. No bounds to his impidence! He might count himself to be a man or – or Somebody – '

A voice the other side of the brook boomed:

> "I wonder who his cloak would turn
> When Puck had led him round,
> Or where those walking fires would burn – "

Then the children went in singing "Farewell, Rewards and Fairies" at the tops of their voices. They had forgotten that they had not even said good-night to Puck.

THE CHILDREN'S SONG

Land of our Birth, we pledge to thee
Our love and toil in the years to be;
When we are grown and take our place
As men and women with our race.

Father in Heaven Who lovest all,
Oh, help Thy children when they call;
That they may build from age to age
An undefilèd heritage.

Teach us to bear the yoke in youth,
With steadfastness and careful truth;
That, in our time, Thy Grace may give
The Truth whereby the Nations live.

Teach us to rule ourselves alway,
Controlled and cleanly night and day;
That we may bring, if need arise,
No maimed or worthless sacrifice.

Teach us to look in all our ends,
On Thee for judge, and not our friends;
That we, with Thee, may walk uncowed
By fear or favour of the crowd.

Teach us the Strength that cannot seek,
By deed or thought, to hurt the weak;
That, under Thee, we may possess
Man's strength to comfort man's distress.

Teach us Delight in simple things,
And Mirth that has no bitter springs;
Forgiveness free of evil done,
And Love to all men 'neath the sun!

Land of our Birth, our faith, our pride,
For whose dear sake our fathers died;
O Motherland, we pledge to thee
Head, heart and hand through the years to be!